OUT OF LUCK . . .

"Eddie? What happened?"

The injured man was only able to gurgle as blood poured from his mouth.

"Eddie—"

There was a rattle, and then the man was still. He was dead, and Clint wondered how he had been able to stagger from the alley with that wound—and, if it had happened shortly after he'd left the game, how he had managed to live this long.

Clint looked around but there was no one on the street to help him. He'd have to leave the body on the street and go back for help. He hated to interrupt the game, but a man was dead.

He headed back for the saloon, hoping that San Sebastian had a sheriff . . .

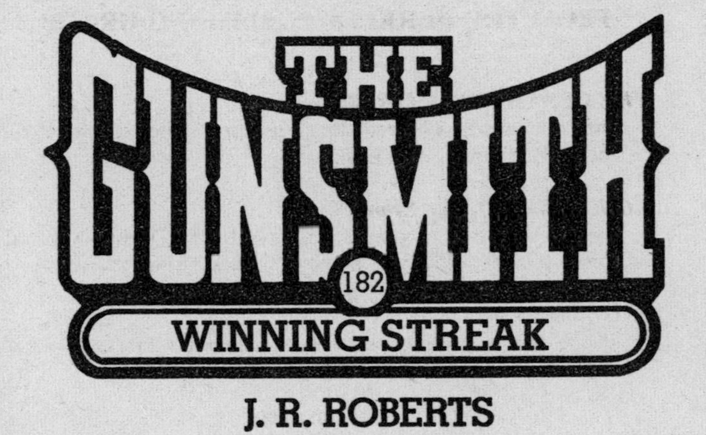

J. R. ROBERTS

JOVE BOOKS, NEW YORK

WINNING STREAK

A Jove Book / published by arrangement with
the author

PRINTING HISTORY
Jove edition / February 1997

The Putnam Berkley World Wide Web site address is
http://www.berkley.com/berkley

ISBN: 0-515-12017-0

A JOVE BOOK®
Jove Books are published by The Berkley Publishing Group,
200 Madison Avenue, New York, New York 10016.
JOVE and the "J" design are trademarks
belonging to Jove Publications, Inc.

PRINTED IN THE UNITED STATES OF AMERICA

10 9 8 7 6 5 4 3 2 1

THE
GUNSMITH
182
WINNING STREAK

PROLOGUE

Ken Witmer looked across the table at the beautiful woman sitting opposite him. The other players had long since bowed out of this hand, but Lindsey Green gave no indication of wavering. Apparently, she thought she had a very good hand. She was obviously unaware of two things. Firstly, that Witmer had a full house—kings over threes—and secondly, that Ken Witmer did not lose pots this big.

"Well," Lindsey said, "I guess it's up to just you and me, Mr. Witmer. I surely hope you don't mind my beginner's luck."

He stared across the table at her and didn't react as she batted her eyelashes at him, giving him the full power of those violet eyes. If she was a beginner then she was also a virgin, and Witmer knew that couldn't be true. The low-cut neckline of her red gown revealed acres of creamy white flesh. He was willing to bet that she was corseted into that dress, not because she needed to be, but because it pushed her cleavage almost up to her chin—and a lovely chin it was, leading down into a graceful, beautiful long neck. Her shoulders were as creamy and smooth as her bosom, and everyone could see that because her dark hair was cut short. She appeared to be in her late twenties, and no woman of that age who looked like that could possibly be a virgin.

And she wasn't a beginner, either. Witmer had long ago determined that Lindsey, while not an out-and-out cheater, was not above using subterfuge to try to throw him off his game. First the innocent oh-I've-never-played-this-game-but-I've-always-wanted-to-learn act, and then add to that the cleavage and eyes, and what man *wouldn't* be distracted?

But you couldn't distract Ken Witmer from his cards for long. He knew damn well what he had in his hands. He had three kings and two threes, and let Lindsey Green try to use her bosom and eyes and shoulders and lips and whatever else to try to distract him from *that.*

"So it seems," he said, "it's just you and me."

They were playing five-card draw, so there were no cards showing at all. He could only guess at what she had, but it was his determination that, as far ahead as she was, she was not above trying to buy this pot. Well, he was ahead, too, and he had plenty of money to stay with her.

"It's your bet, Mr. Witmer," Lindsey Green said, smiling sweetly.

"Yes, I know it's my bet, Miss Green," Witmer said. "Thank you very much for reminding me."

"Your mind seems to be wandering, Mr. Witmer," Lindsey said. "That's not a good thing in poker, is it?"

"Never mind," Witmer said, "my mind is right here with these cards, Miss Green. I bet five hundred."

There was a collective gasp from the crowd of onlookers. That was the largest bet of the night.

"You must be very confident of your cards, Mr. Witmer," she said.

"I'm five hundred dollars confident," he said. "Are you?"

"Oh, yes," she said, "I'm your five hundred confident and . . ."—she looked down at her chips, then started pushing them into the pot—"three thousand more."

Ha, Witmer thought, he had her now. He could easily match her three thousand and raise her another two and she didn't have any more chips left in front of her.

"That's pretty confident," he said.

She smiled, raised her eyebrows, and nodded, all from behind her cards.

"I tell you what," Witmer said, "I'll just call your three thousand and raise you another two."

Lindsey looked aghast.

"But I don't have any more chips."

"Then you can't see the bet," Witmer said, placing his cards down on the table and preparing to rake in the pot. "I win."

"But—that's not fair."

"That is poker, madam," Witmer said. "You play with what you bring to the table."

"Wait—" she said as he reached for the chips.

"What? Do you have something else with you?"

"I do."

"What?"

She raised her chin and said, "Me."

Witmer laughed. A man who appreciated a beautiful woman, he'd always been able to separate business from pleasure when it came to a time like this.

"Sorry," he said, "I only take cash."

Lindsey glared at him, then looked over at Lucas Richaud. She was aware that the Frenchman had been watching her the whole evening.

"Madame," Richaud said, in an accent Witmer was convinced was a phony.

"Monsieur Richaud?" Lindsey said.

The man smiled.

"I would perhaps be interested in backing your play, madame, but . . ."

"But what?"

"I would have to . . . see the merchandise first. You understand, of course."

"Of course," Lindsey said. She looked at Witmer and said, "Just give me a few minutes."

"May we use your office?" Richaud asked Witmer.

"Sure," Witmer said, "go ahead. Be my guest."

Richaud was a big-bellied bear of a Frenchman who wore fine suits as if they were buckskin. His ruffled shirts always seemed to be getting in his face, and his hair and mustache must have been blackened in some artificial way. Witmer had enjoyed taking his money all night, but he was also aware that Richaud was a wealthy man—and that he didn't like one Ken Witmer.

He watched as the two walked to his office and entered.

In the office no words were spoken. Lindsey walked to the center of the room, turned, and shrugged off her dress. Richaud was surprised at how quickly it happened.

"You have a minute," she said, standing there naked, with her hands on her hips.

Richaud's mouth went dry at the sight of her. He liked beautiful women, but they did not like him. He was a man who frequented whorehouses for his pleasures, but never had a whorehouse offered him anything like Lindsey Green.

Her breasts were larger than he would have thought, and very firm. Her skin was smooth and pale, her legs long and lovely. His eyes took in all of her, her navel, the tangle of hair between her legs. She even turned slowly so that he could see her high, firm buttocks.

"That's it," she said abruptly. She bent over, retrieved her gown from the floor, and put it back on.

"What's the verdict?"

"I will back your play, madame. Eh, how much?"

"Ten thousand."

Richaud was surprised.

"Ten thousand dollars is a lot of money."

"You get me," she said, "and the satisfaction of seeing Ken Witmer beaten . . . by a woman."

Richaud smiled.

"You drive a hard bargain, madame."

"We have a deal?"

He nodded.

"We have a deal."

"I call your two and raise eight thousand."

"Eight thousand?" Witmer said, glaring at Richaud, who only smiled. He'd been smiling since he and Lindsey had returned from his office. "I don't have eight thousand."

"Boo-hoo," Lindsey said without a trace of pity, "then I guess I win—that is, unless you brought something else to the table?"

Witmer glared at her and at Richaud in turn, then reached his hand into his pocket, only to come out empty.

"I need something to write on," he shouted, "and something to write with."

The bartender appeared with a piece of paper and a pencil.

"A marker?" Lindsey asked. "I'm not going to accept your marker."

"This is not a marker," Witmer said, continuing to write frantically. "This will act as a deed for this saloon, and everything in it."

Now there was another sharp intake of breath.

He looked up at her and said, "It's worth a helluva lot more than eight thousand dollars."

"Boss," the bartender said, "you sure you wanna do that?"

"Shut up, Culley. Well?"

Lindsey let him swing a bit in the breeze, tapping her bottom lip with a dainty pinky before she finally said, "All right, I'll accept your bet—but only to call, not to raise."

"I only want to call," Witmer said, smiling tightly and dropping the deed into the pot. "This has to come to a stop sometime."

"Indeed it does," Lindsey said, and spread her cards on the table.

ONE

Two years later . . .

When Clint rode into San Sebastian, Texas, he thought that it was an unremarkable place for a group of high rollers to get together for a poker game. The fact that the weather was rainy and the streets muddy did not dress it up any. San Sebastian was a small, run-down town not far from the Mexican border. Anybody who came here to play poker would not have much of anything else to do.

Clint Adams, poker enthusiast that he was, had not come to play, he had come to watch. He knew of the game, but he did not know which players were coming. He assumed that he would see some of his friends here, but if he didn't that was fine, too. First and foremost he was here to see five or six or more men passing great sums of money around a poker table.

One man Clint did know would be here was Ken Witmer.

For want of a better word, Witmer would have to be described as a friend. Clint had known him for over ten years. The man was a gambler, and had all the makings of a good one. He especially had the nerve to gamble big, which meant that when he won and lost, he did so in a big way. For that reason Witmer had been rich and poor many times over. His only downfall was his ego. Had he been a more even-tempered man, he might have become rich and stayed that way, but his ego would never let him rest. He was constantly trying to prove to others—and to himself—that he was the greatest gambler, and best poker player, who ever lived. While the man was good, Clint would never have described him as the best, not while the likes of Luke Short and Bat Masterson and some others were still around.

Clint rode Duke to the livery and gave him over to the liveryman's care.

"You here for the game?" the man asked.

"I am."

"To play, or to watch?"

"To watch."

"They don't let too many people watch."

"I was invited." Clint took his gear and left the livery, feeling he didn't have to explain any more to the man.

The liveryman watched him leave and wondered who he was. He had to be somebody to have been invited to watch the game—and to have such a magnificent horse.

Clint's invitation, which had come to Labyrinth, Texas, by telegram, also told him that a room would be held for him at the San Sebastian Hotel. The hotel, he was surprised to find, had three floors and was not in as bad condition as most of the other buildings in town. He wondered if it had been fixed up specifically for this event. The chances were good that all of the players would also be housed there.

Clint entered and approached the front desk. The lobby was bare, but it was clean. The desk clerk, a youngish-looking man with slicked-down hair, smiled at him.

"Can I help you?"

"Yes," Clint said, "I'd like a room."

"Are you here for the game, sir?"

"Yes."

"And your name?"

"Clint Adams."

"One moment, sir."

The man consulted a list of names and satisfied himself that Clint was on it.

"Yes, sir, you have room fourteen, one flight up." The man handed him a key. "Do you need help with any baggage?"

"No, thanks."

"Mr. Witmer left a message, sir, asking if you would join him in the saloon when you arrived."

"All right."

"Have a nice stay, sir."

"I will."

"Just go to the head of the stairs and make a right, sir."

Clint nodded, took his saddlebags and rifle, and went up the stairs to the second floor. He found fourteen and entered. It was clean, with a decent bed, a dresser with a pitcher and basin on top, and one wooden chair.

He dropped the saddlebags and rifle on the bed and walked to the window. His room overlooked an alley, but he could see part of the main street from it. He looked straight down and saw that the alley was empty, except for some rain puddles.

He touched his hand to his mouth and realized that he wanted a beer very badly. He hadn't had the opportunity to send a telegram back to Ken Witmer, mainly because he wasn't even sure where the original one had come from. The telegram had suggested, however, that he arrive on this day, the day before the game. Since Witmer was expecting him to arrive today, and wanted to meet him in the saloon, he wondered if the man had been there the whole afternoon, waiting for him.

He figured he'd better get over there before Witmer was too drunk to recognize him.

TWO

Clint went back down to the lobby and asked the clerk what saloon Ken Witmer was meeting him in.

''We've only got one,'' the clerk said. ''You can't miss it. It's called the San Sebastian Saloon.''

''I think I'll be able to find it.''

He left the hotel and found the saloon with no problem. When he entered he saw that it was kind of empty, which was surprising for that time of day. Only three tables were occupied, and there were two men standing at the bar. Ken Witmer was sitting at one of the tables with three other men playing—what else—poker. At least he knew the man was sober, because Witmer—like Clint—did not drink while playing. Clint thought that this was an exceptionally smart move on Witmer's part. His ego was already big enough, but if he played drunk it would be out of control.

Clint walked in and stopped at the bar to get a beer. He

was walking toward the poker table when Witmer looked up and saw him.

"Clint! You made it. Deal me out, boys."

"You got all our money," one of the men complained.

Picking up his winnings, Witmer said, "Poker lessons don't come cheap, my friends."

He tucked his money away, needing several pockets to do it, and threw one arm around Clint's shoulder.

"Let's go to the bar and I'll buy you a drink. Oh, you have a drink. Okay, then let's go to the bar and buy me a drink."

Witmer was in his late thirties, with dark hair and a smooth, handsome face. He was not tall, and was built along slender lines. Women liked him, and he liked them—except when he was gambling.

"Bartender, a beer," Witmer said when they reached the bar. Then he turned to Clint and slapped him on the back. "How the hell are you? It's been a while."

"Year and a half, maybe more."

"Probably more," Witmer said, turning to accept his beer. "I've been moving around a lot."

"So have I."

"Not such that you didn't get my telegram in Labyrinth. Is that turning into your home away from home?"

"Maybe."

"For how long?"

"Who knows?"

"I can't stay in one place for long myself. I get restless."

"I know that."

"So what do you think of this place, huh?"

"The saloon?"

"The saloon, the town. The whole place."

"It's . . . unimpressive. Not the kind of place I'd usually find you."

"That's where you're wrong," Witmer said, putting his beer down. "You know why? I'll tell you why. This town is gonna grow."

"It is?"

"Yes, it is. This town is gonna grow and I want to be part of it."

"Why?"

Witmer shrugged and said, "Oh, maybe I'm thinking about settling down."

Clint stared at his friend and said, "There's a woman involved in this decision somewhere, isn't there?"

"Well . . . yes, and no."

"What's that mean?"

"It means that there is a woman, but she's only part of the reason."

"What's the other part?"

"Money."

"That's always a consideration with you."

"Don't make me sound so mercenary," Witmer said. "Money is a consideration with everybody, even you—okay, on a smaller scale with you, but still with you, you've got to admit."

"Sometimes."

They each finished their beers and Witmer said, "I'll buy you another one."

"Fine."

They got two more and Witmer said, "Come with me."

"Where?"

"Just to a table. I want to talk to you."

"Uh-oh."

"What do you mean, uh-oh?"

"There's a pitch coming."

"What? What pitch?"

"That's what I'm wondering. There's some kind of offer coming here."

"Just come with me to a table."

"Is there really a poker game in town, Ken? Or was that a ruse to get me here?"

"There's a game, a big game, don't worry."

"Who's playing?"

"Come and sit."

"Tell me who's playing."

"Jesus, don't you trust me?"

"When you want something," Clint said, "you're very untrustworthy."

"Who's playing?" Witmer repeated. "I'll tell you who's playing. I'll give you one name, and if you like it you'll come and sit down, okay?"

"What's the name?"

"Bat Masterson."

"Bat's coming?"

"He's coming. He's your best friend, right?"

"Well . . ."

"He's coming, don't worry," Witmer said, "and lots of other guys. Now come and sit and talk, okay?"

Grudgingly, Clint said, "Okay."

THREE

''Well,'' Clint said, sitting opposite Witmer with his back to the wall, ''make your play.''

''Why are you so suspicious?''

''Because I know you, that's why,'' Clint said. ''You're as much con man as gambler.''

''Oh, that was the old me,'' Witmer said. ''This is the new me.''

''Yeah, well,'' Clint said, ''I've known three or four of the new you, Kenny.''

''No, this time I mean it,'' Witmer said, moving his chair closer to the table. ''I've turned over a new leaf, and this place is the result.''

Clint looked around and then said, ''This place?''

''Yes,'' Witmer said. ''Oh, not the way it looks now. I'm gonna fix it up.''

''Why?''

''I told you why,'' Witmer said. ''This town is gonna

boom, and I want to be here when it does.''

''Ken, if you want to buy this place I don't guess I could stop you—''

''You can't,'' Witmer said with a satisfied look on his face, ''because I already bought it.''

''You did?''

Witmer nodded.

''And I'm going to start fixing it up.''

''When?''

''Right after I win this poker game.''

''Is that what this is about?'' Clint asked. ''You put this game together so you'd have the money to fix this place up?''

''Well, I used all the money I had to buy it. I had nothing left to use to redo it.''

''And you expect to win the money for it.''

''Well, sure. Why not?''

''And you invited Bat Masterson to play?''

''Yes.''

''And who else?''

''Well, I invited Ben Thompson, and Luke Short, Dick Clark, Doc Holliday—''

''You invited Doc?''

''Why not?''

''Because Doc wouldn't put up with your shenanigans, that's why. You want to get killed?''

''Don't worry,'' Witmer said. ''I also invited Doc Kennedy.''

''What?'' Clint asked, ''Are you crazy?''

''Why?''

''Doc Holliday and Doc Kennedy hate each other. Jesus, everybody knows that.''

''Well, I don't,'' Witmer said. ''Why do they hate each other?''

''Well, Doc Kennedy is always ragging on Doc Holliday because he's a dentist, and not a real doctor.''

''And?''

''And Holliday never lets Kennedy forget that he's a vet, not a people doctor.''

''Well, the whole thing sounds silly, but don't worry,'' Witmer said, ''Doc can't come.''

''Kennedy?''

''Holliday.''

''What about the others?''

''Well, Luke can't make it, and neither can Ben or Dick—''

''Kenny,'' Clint said, cutting him off, ''tell me who *is* coming.''

''Okay,'' Witmer said, ''well, Bat, Jim Everett—''

''*Gentleman* Jim Everett,'' Clint reminded him. ''Don't forget that, or you still might end up dead.''

''Okay, okay,'' Witmer said, ''jeez, these fellas and their nicknames. I don't see you demanding to be called the Gun—''

''Kenny!''

''All right. There's Bat, there's *Gentleman* Jim, there's *One-eyed* Dan Dugan, *Fat* Eddie Gilbert—''

''Don't call him that to his face,'' Clint warned.

''Oh, I forgot, he doesn't want to be called by his nickname. See? That's why I need you.''

''Why?''

''To keep me from getting killed.''

''You asked me to come here to be your bodyguard?''

''No,'' Witmer said, ''well, yes—I mean, yes and no.''

''What *do* you mean, Kenny?''

''I asked you here to be my partner.''

''Partner,'' Clint said.

''Right.''

"And I suppose I'd have to invest some money?"

"Well, of course."

"How much?"

"I don't know," Witmer said. "I suppose that would depend on how much I win."

"Why do you need my money?" Clint asked.

"I need your money so you'll have some vested interest in the place," Witmer said, "but what I really need is you."

"What for?"

"Because you have the temperament to be successful and I don't."

"Come on, Kenny," Clint said. "You've been successful over and over again."

"Yes," Witmer said, "and I've gone bust over and over again. Why is that, Clint?"

"Well—"

"Don't be kind," Witmer said, cutting him off before he could speak, "tell the truth. Why do you think every enterprise I've started has been successful, and then gone bust?"

"Well, Kenny," Clint said, "you can't stand the prosperity. Every time you find yourself on top of the world you find some way to slip to the bottom again."

"I do, don't I? Why is that?"

Clint hesitated, took a deep breath, and said, "Ego."

"Ego?" That was obviously not a word Witmer was expecting to hear.

"Yes."

Witmer frowned.

"What do you mean?"

"You think you can't fail," Clint said, "therefore you do."

"See? That's why I need you."

"Why?"

"To keep me from failing again."

"Kenny, I can't keep you from failing," Clint said, "only you can do that."

"I don't know how," Witmer said.

"You more than anyone I know, Kenny . . . you *know* how to succeed."

"But I don't know how to *stay* successful," Witmer said. "Don't you see? Together we could become successful and stay successful."

"Kenny—"

"A year."

"What?"

"I'd need you for a year," Witmer said. "After that I think I could do it on my own."

"A year . . ." Clint shook his head.

"You wouldn't have to stay here that whole time," Witmer said. "You could come and go, just as long as I knew I had to answer to you. Clint, I've never had a partner before. I've never had someone else to answer to. That's what I need."

"But why me? Why not someone else?"

"I don't respect anyone else."

That made Clint pause.

"Say that again?"

"I said I don't respect anyone else enough to ask them to be my partner."

"Kenny," Clint said, "if you're conning me—"

"I'm not, Clint," Witmer said, "I swear. There's more, though."

"What more?"

Now Witmer hesitated before saying, "There's also no one else I'm afraid of."

"You're afraid of me?"

"Yes . . . oh, not the way a lot of people are afraid of you because of your reputation. I'm afraid of doing something that would . . . well, ruin our friendship."

"Kenny, you've conned me plenty of times before."

"Yes," Witmer said, "but never so badly that you weren't able to forgive me."

"Well . . . well, that's true."

"See?" Witmer said. "I'll need you, Clint, to keep me focused."

"And after a year?"

"If I can go a year without self-destructing I think I'll be all right."

"And after that?" Clint asked again.

"I'll buy you out at a profit."

"What if I don't want to be bought out?"

Witmer grew excited.

"You mean you'll do it?"

"I didn't say that," Clint corrected him. "I'm just exploring all the possibilities."

"Hey, if you don't want to sell out you won't have to."

Clint sat back in his chair, amazed that he was even considering this, but as long as he had known Kenny Witmer he had never seen him actually build a success. He'd seen him lose them, but never build them, and he'd always wondered how he did it.

"You know," he said, "if you didn't have an ego you'd be a man with a Midas touch."

"So be the one who cures me of it," Witmer said. "What do you say?"

"I'll have to think about it, Kenny," Clint said, annoyed at himself. "I'll have to think about it long and hard."

"Hey, we've got time," Witmer said. "The other players won't start arriving until tomorrow, the game starts the next day, and who knows how long it will go on. We've got time. I'm just glad you're going to give it some thought."

"A *lot* of thought," Clint said.

"Right," Witmer said, lifting his beer mug, "here's to a lot of thought."

FOUR

They had another beer and Clint asked about the woman in Witmer's life.

"She's Mexican."

"Ah," Clint said, "that's why you picked a town near the border."

"Well, yeah," Witmer said, "that's one reason, but I also picked San Sebastian for some other reasons."

"Like what?"

"Well, don't you want to hear about Carmen?"

"Carmen."

"Yeah, that's her name, Carmen," Witmer said. "You asked about the woman."

"Okay, tell me about Carmen."

"Oh, she's beautiful," Witmer said. "Lots of black hair, black eyes, beautiful body. She's young, only twenty-three—"

"Twenty-three?"

"Yeah, you don't think she's too young for me, do you? I'm . . . thirty-three."

"I thought you were thirty-six."

Witmer grinned.

"Well, actually I'm thirty-seven, but I told her I was thirty-three."

"And her father?"

"Uh, yeah, I told her father, too."

"And who's he?"

"He's this big rancher in Mexico. Got this big spread not far from here. His name is Don Carlos Dominguez . . . uh, a bunch of other names, and then Ortiz."

"Why don't you settle on that side of the river, Kenny?"

"I thought about that, Clint," Witmer said, "but I'm American, you know? This is my home."

"And what about Carmen? Will she be able to settle here?"

Witmer looked sheepish.

"To tell you the truth, I haven't asked her yet. I mean, I haven't asked her to marry me."

"Why not?"

"Because I don't have anything to offer her," Witmer said. "But soon, with your help, I will."

Clint frowned.

"That's not fair."

"I know," Witmer said, "but I just thought I'd throw it in. A little pressure never hurt anybody."

"Are you really planning on asking her to marry you?" Clint asked.

"Yes," Witmer said, "just as soon as I have this place going."

"Tell me about the game," Clint said, wanting to change the subject.

"You don't think I can do it, do you?"

"Do what?"

"Settle down."

"Kenny . . ."

"Come on, Clint," Witmer said, "I already told you I want the truth."

"You've never given any indication that this is something you wanted to do."

"Well," Witmer said, "I'm giving it now."

"Look," Clint said, a bit helplessly, "I'll help you all I can, but I don't know if I can give you a year."

"Think it over."

"I already told you I would," Clint said. "Why don't you tell me about the game?"

They talked a bit about who was playing, and who Witmer saw as his main competition. Of course, he feared Bat Masterson, but he wasn't that worried about the other players.

"I suppose you're wondering why I didn't invite you to play."

"No," Clint said. "You're under no obligation to invite me. Besides, I'm not in the same class as some of those others."

"What? No, that's not why I didn't invite you."

"Oh?" In spite of himself Clint asked, "Then why didn't you?"

"I told you already," Witmer said. "I respect you. I didn't want to have to go up against you for this money."

Clint stared at Witmer and then said, "Come on—"

"No, I'm serious," Witmer said.

"Then why invite Bat?"

"Well," Witmer said, "I want *some* competition."

Clint didn't think it was possible that Witmer thought he could beat Bat Masterson but not him.

''Well,'' Witmer said, ''I better get going. I've still got preparations to make.''

''Where's the game going to be held?''

''Right here,'' Witmer said. ''Gonna clear the place out and put some tables right in the center of the room.''

''And close for business?''

''Why not?'' Witmer asked. ''If I win, it'll be worth it.''

''What if you lose, Kenny?''

Witmer made a face.

''I don't even want to think about that, Clint. Where are you gonna be?''

''Where else is there to go?''

''No place but here, or the hotel.''

''And to eat?''

''Stay in the hotel for that,'' Witmer said, ''it's safer.''

''Thanks for the advice.''

''Oh,'' Witmer said, ''and there's a whorehouse.''

''Uh-huh.''

''There's one or two girls that are worth a visit.''

''That's okay.''

''Oh, I forgot,'' Witmer said, ''you don't pay for it. Still don't?''

''Still don't.''

''Well, I won't either, once I'm married,'' the other man said, then added, ''maybe.''

As Ken Witmer went out the door, Clint wondered what the odds would be if he was taking bets on whether or not his friend would really be able to settle down.

High, very high.

FIVE

Don Carlos Dominguez Velez Colon Ortiz sat in the plush chair behind his desk in his den and thought about Ken Witmer. He looked around the room. The den was the only part of the house that reflected his taste. The rest of the house had been decorated and furnished by his late wife. When she died he swore on her grave that he would never change anything. This, then, was his sanctuary and he resented the American for intruding on it, even if it was only in his thoughts.

There was a knock on the door and Don Carlos said, "*Venga.*"

The door opened and two men entered. Both were vaqueros on Don Carlos's ranch, but the task he had in mind for them had nothing to do with ranching.

"Don Carlos?" Jesus Mendez said. "You sent for us?"

"Yes, Jesus, I did," Ortiz said. "*Cera la puerta.*"

Mendez did as he was told and closed the door. He and

the other man, Tino Rosario, inched closer to their *patrón*'s desk.

"I have a job for you both."

"*Sí, Patrón,*" Mendez said. "We will do whatever you say."

"I understand that you both did other things before you came to work for me six months ago."

"*Sí, Patrón,*" Mendez said, "but they were sinful things."

"What kind of things?"

"We lied, we stole, we did bad things, *Patrón.*"

Rosario nodded enthusiastically.

Both men were in their mid-thirties. They were ugly, dirty men whom Ortiz had hired when he was in dire straits and needed all the men he could muster. Lately, however, he had been thinking about getting rid of them. They were not the kind of men he usually liked to have working at his rancho.

They were, however, perfect for the job he now had in mind.

"Did you ever kill anyone?"

Mendez lowered his head and said, "*Sí*, we have killed. But we have repented, *Patrón*. We do not do those things anymore."

"Do you like working here?"

"*Sí, Patrón,*" Mendez said, "we like it very much."

"Are you grateful that I took you on here?"

"*Sí, Patrón*, very grateful."

"Then it is time for you to pay me back."

"We would be honored."

"I want you to kill a man for me."

"*Patrón?*" Both men looked confused.

"He has dishonored my name, and my daughter," Ortiz said. "This is very important to me, do you understand?"

"*Sí, Patrón,*" Mendez said, "we understand, and we would be honored to do this thing, but . . . but we have repented. We do not . . . murder anymore."

Ortiz sat back and regarded the two men. Murderers, in his opinion, did not change. If the men had repented, it was a temporary thing. They were simply waiting for the right moment to revert back to their murderous ways.

And he was going to give it to them.

"I can trust no one else with this task," he said gravely. "If you do not do this for me, it will go undone. Do you understand? The man who has besmirched my honor will go unpunished."

The two men looked at each other and something passed between them.

"*Patrón,*" Mendez finally said, "we will do this thing for you. Tell us who this man is, and he is a dead man."

"His name is Ken Witmer. Do you know him?"

"*Sí, Patrón,*" Mendez said, frowning, "he was a guest here only a few weeks ago."

"Yes, he was."

"Was this when he dishonored the señorita?"

"It is."

"Under your own roof?"

"Yes."

"*Hijo de un cabrón y una puta!*" Mendez spat.

"Yes," Ortiz said, "he is the son of a pimp and a whore. This is why I wish you to kill him."

"It will be done, *Patrón,*" Mendez said. "You have only to tell us where he is and it will be done."

"I know exactly where he is," Ortiz said. "He is in San Sebastian, on the other side of the river, in *los Estados Unidos*. Will you go there?"

"*Sí,*" Mendez said, "we will go there and do this thing for the honor of our *patrón.*"

"Good," Ortiz said, "very good—and Jesus?"

"*Sí?*"

"You must tell no one of this, do you understand? No one!"

"*Sí, Patrón,*" Mendez said, "we understand."

"*Bueno,*" Ortiz said. "I knew I would be able to count on you. Go now. When you return you will be rewarded."

Ortiz watched as the two men left his den and knew that if his daughter ever found out about this she would hate him forever, but he would not and could not let her marry this gringo. He was a gambler, and a dishonorable man, and he would break her heart.

And Don Carlos would not see this man lay one hand on his holdings when he died and it all passed to his daughter.

Mendez and Rosario left Carlos Ortiz's house and went directly to the barn to saddle their horses. They would go directly to San Sebastian and await their opportunity to avenge their *patrón*.

As they led their horses from the bar, Rosario spoke for the first time.

"Jesus?"

"Yes?"

"This thing we are to do?"

"Yes."

"It is a bad thing, is it not?"

"*Sí*, Tino, it is a bad thing."

"A very bad thing?"

"A very bad thing."

"And it is all right for us to do it?"

"It is all right," Mendez said, "because our *patrón* has asked us to do it."

Rosario nodded, and they mounted up.

"Jesus?"

"*Sí*, Tino?"

With a smile that revealed either gold or rotten teeth, Rosario said, "I have missed doing very bad things."

Mendez looked at his friend, smiled, and said, "So have I, amigo. So have I."

SIX

Clint had breakfast in the hotel the next morning, where he'd had dinner the night before. The waiter had just brought him his food when Ken Witmer entered the dining room and came over to his table.

"Well, today's the day," he said, sitting opposite Clint.

"You going to start it with a good breakfast?"

Witmer waved the waiter over and said, "Coffee, lots of it." The waiter walked away and Witmer looked at Clint. "No food, just coffee. I'm too excited."

"You better control that excitement if you want to win this game."

"Oh, once the game starts I'll be fine."

"You better be," Clint said. "You won't be able to play well if you're all wound up like this, and it sounds like your basing your future on this game."

"I am," Witmer said. "No, don't worry. It's just the anticipation. Once the cards are dealt I'll be fine."

"Do you have dealers?"

"Yeah, three of 'em."

"Who'd you get?"

"Three of the best."

Clint wondered silently why he hadn't asked this question last night.

"Who? Ace Bannister?"

"No."

"Jack Willis?"

"No."

"Eric Patch?"

"No."

"I'm finished guessing, Kenny."

"Waco Muldoon."

Clint winced.

"Muldoon's a loose cannon, Kenny."

"He'll be fine."

"He wears a gun at the table."

"He'll be fine," Witmer said again.

"Who else?"

"Jo Dillon."

"Jesus," Clint said, "I haven't seen Jo in years."

"She still looks great."

"She must be . . ."

"Fifty?"

"I wasn't going to guess that high."

"She's still a handsome woman."

"And who's the third dealer?"

"Kendall Will."

Clint frowned.

"I don't know the name."

"He's been dealing for about three or four years," Witmer said. "Maybe you haven't crossed paths with him."

"I guess not. What about security?"

Witmer didn't answer right away.

"Do you have any security, Kenny?" Clint asked. "It sounds like there's going to be a lot of money on these tables."

"Well," Witmer said, "that was something else I wanted to talk to you about."

"Uh-huh," Clint said. "Something you couldn't bring up yesterday, huh?"

"Well, I didn't want to hit you with too much at one time. I, uh, didn't have any money to hire security."

"So you want me to do it?"

"Well," Witmer said sheepishly, "since you're here."

"Kenny," Clint said, "you conned me again."

"I didn't," Witmer said, "I swear. I thought I'd have enough money to hire somebody like Heck Thomas or . . . or somebody like that, but I didn't—and I had already invited you. If you don't want to do it, I'll understand."

"And if I don't do it, who will?"

"Well," Witmer said, "all the players will have guns . . ."

"Kenny, you know guns at a poker table is asking for trouble."

"I know, but—"

"Never mind," Clint said. "I'll keep an eye on things."

"I could pay you after I win," Witmer said, "that is, unless you agree to be partners—"

"Let's put that off until afterward, okay?" Clint said.

"Okay. Thanks, Clint, I owe you."

The waiter came with a cup and another pot of coffee.

"Players should start arriving today."

"You gave them one day to get here?"

"They all have to be here by midnight tonight. I'm surprised some of them haven't already arrived ahead of time."

"Maybe they know something about what San Sebastian has to offer."

"Hey," Witmer said, "we've got a whorehouse."

"Kenny," Clint said, "you wouldn't happen to have a piece of the whorehouse, would you?"

"Well," Witmer said, looking into his cup, "maybe a small piece."

"I thought so."

"As soon as I win, I'll arrange for some new girls, don't worry. But like I told you, we do have one or two decent ones over there."

"Never mind."

Clint ate his breakfast while Witmer consumed cup after cup of coffee. Finally, Witmer pushed his chair back.

"I'm going to go outside and sit awhile, maybe watch the players ride in. They'll be arriving all day."

"I'll come with you," Clint said, "after I finish my coffee."

"Okay," Witmer said, standing up. "I'm really excited about this, Clint. When the first card is dealt, the rest of my life will begin."

Clint was of the opinion, win or lose, that would happen when the last card was dealt, but he kept his opinion to himself.

SEVEN

When Clint came outside, Witmer was sitting in a wooden chair with his back to the wall. There was an empty chair next to him.

"Anybody get here yet?"

"No."

Clint studied his friend's profile.

"What are you worried about, Kenny?"

Witmer bit his lip, then answered without looking at Clint.

"What if nobody comes?"

"Why would nobody come, Kenny?"

"You haven't heard much from me in a few years, have you, Clint?"

"Well, no, I haven't."

"You ever think about me?"

"Sure."

"Wonder where I was, what I was doing?"

"Yes."

"Well, I wasn't doing too good."

Clint decided to remain silent and let Witmer tell it in his own time.

"I was a drunk."

Clint waited, then knew he'd have to prompt his friend.

"For how long?"

"Off and on . . . two years."

"What? Why didn't you get in touch with me?"

"For what? So you could talk me out of it?"

"Yes."

"I didn't want to be talked out of it."

"How long has it been since you had a drink?"

"I had those two beers with you yesterday. That was the first in four months."

"Have you had one since?"

"No."

"You seemed . . . all right, drinking it."

"I didn't want to drink it," Witmer said, "I wanted to dive in and pull it in after me."

After a moment of silence, Clint asked, "What happened?"

"Do you know a woman named Lindsey Green?"

"I've heard the name," Clint said, "but I never met her."

"I had a place in Sumner, Missouri, a beautiful saloon and gambling place I called the Palace."

"Original."

"Okay, so I'm not good at picking names," Witmer said. "I made a success of the place."

"I don't doubt that. What happened?"

"I lost it, on one hand of poker."

"To Lindsey Green?"

"Yes . . . the bitch."

"Did she cheat?"

"I thought so for a long time," Witmer said, "but I finally had to admit to myself that she hadn't. It was my fault, my ego wouldn't allow me to believe that a woman could beat me, not when I had kings full over threes."

Clint whistled and said, "Nice hand."

"It wins most of the time," Witmer said, "except when your opponent has aces full over deuces."

Clint whistled again.

"She took my place and rubbed it in my face," Witmer said. "I've seen bad losers before, but that woman was the worst winner I've ever seen."

"I've known a few men like that."

"Yeah, well," Witmer said, "somehow the fact that it was a woman made it worse."

"And that's when you started drinking?"

"Yeah. You know, I've met a lot of men who were driven to drunkenness by a woman, but at least they got to sleep with them first."

"And you think the word got out about this?"

"I figured."

"I didn't hear about it," Clint said, "and I usually keep my ear to the ground. Maybe you're worried for no reason."

"I hope so."

After a moment Clint said, "So you dried out."

"Yeah, in Mexico," Witmer said. "Carmen helped me a lot. She sees something in me that nobody else sees. That's what's made me want to settle down here, build myself a place that I can keep."

Clint looked at his friend for a long time. Witmer finally felt his gaze and turned to return it.

"You know, Kenny," Clint said, "you *have* changed. Maybe this time you will make it stick."

"Will you help me?"

Clint thought a moment, then nodded and said, "I'll help you."

"Thanks."

After a moment Clint added, "If you're conning me . . ."

"No con, Clint," Witmer said, looking at him. "I swear. Okay?"

Clint returned his friend's look, nodded, and said, "Okay."

"Here come some riders," Witmer said excitedly. "Let's see who they are."

EIGHT

"I should have known you'd show up first," Clint said to Bat Masterson.

Bat looked down at Clint and Ken Witmer from his horse and said, "First? I thought I'd be fashionably late."

"Hello, Bat."

"Hello, Ken. Didn't know you'd be here, Clint. Are you playing?"

Clint shook his head.

"Just watching."

Bat nodded, then looked at Witmer.

"Where can I leave my horse?"

"Livery's around the corner. You'll be staying in this hotel. Game's in the saloon you passed on the way in."

"Quaint town," Bat said, looking around.

"It'll grow."

"Buy you a drink later?" Bat asked Clint.

"Sure."

"See you."

Bat rode his horse around the corner toward the livery. Clint and Witmer reclaimed their chairs.

"He doesn't like me," Witmer said.

"What makes you say that?"

"He never says more than he has to to me."

"He's like that with everybody."

"Not with you."

"He likes me."

Witmer nodded.

"My point is made."

After a few minutes Bat came walking around the corner with his saddlebags and a rifle.

"Saloon in half an hour?" he asked Clint.

"I'll be there."

Bat went into the hotel.

"What happened to those other two?" Witmer wondered after a while.

Before Bat had arrived, two other riders had come to town. They were Mexicans, and obviously not there for the game, so there'd been no reason to talk to them. They had ridden past them, and had not been seen since.

"Is there another place to stay in town?" Clint asked.

"Just a boardinghouse."

"Maybe they went there, then."

"Yeah, maybe."

They were silent for a while.

"Somebody else comin' in," Witmer said.

"Looks like your people are starting to arrive," Clint said. "I'll leave you to greet them. I've got to meet Bat at the saloon."

"I'll see you later."

Clint got up and walked down toward the saloon. On the way he passed the rider, who he didn't recognize. Once he was past the man, he crossed over and looked back at him. Witmer was out in the middle of the street, greeting the man with a smile, so he was obviously a player.

Clint entered the saloon, which only had about three other customers in it. He got a beer from the bartender and offered to pay.

"Your money's no good here," the man said. "You're a friend of the boss."

"I might be a little more than that."

"Partner?"

Clint nodded.

"Then you are the boss," the man said, sticking out his hand. "Name's Culley."

Clint shook the man's hand. He was tall, over six feet, with a bit of a gut. He had his sleeves rolled up over hairy, huge forearms. He looked to be in his late thirties.

"Boxer?" Clint asked.

"Wrestler," the man said. "I could never fight, but I could wrestle."

"Have you known Kenny long?"

"Not long enough to call him Kenny," the man said, "but long enough to have worked for him a few times when he had other places."

"What do you think about this place?"

"I've seen worse," Culley said, "but not much worse. Still, he has a way with places, ya know?"

"Yes, I know," Clint said, and then a thought struck him. "Did you work for him in Sumner?"

Culley nodded gravely.

"Were you there . . ."

"The night that gal took the place from him? I was there. He was never the same after that."

"Did you work for her?"

The man shook his head.

"I quit about one second ahead of being fired. I heard she cleaned house and hired all her own people."

"Had you seen Ken since?"

"Hadn't heard from or seen him, not until he wired me to meet him here."

"And you came?"

"He's always been a good boss," Culley said. "Why not?"

"You any good with a gun, Culley?"

"Shotgun's about all," Culley said. "I keep it behind the bar."

"Good," Clint said. "Keep it handy. I'm handling security for the game, and I might have to depend on you for some help."

"I'll be right here," Culley said.

"Thanks."

Clint walked to the back table he'd shared with Witmer before and sat down to await Bat's arrival.

NINE

"Why can't we stay at the hotel?" Rosario asked Mendez.

"Because, *estúpido*, that is where the gringo will be staying. We will stay at the boardinghouse the man at the livery told us about."

Rosario nudged his friend and said, "He also told us about the whorehouse, eh?"

"You will have your *puta*, do not worry," Mendez said, "but also do not forget why we are here."

Tino Rosario's face turned very solemn and grave, and he said, "We are here to do a bad thing, a very bad thing."

And both men laughed.

When Bat entered the saloon he stopped just inside the door to look around—which didn't take long. Including Clint, there were still only four men in the place. He went to the bar, got a beer, and joined Clint at his table.

"A little early for this town?" he asked.

"I think it might always be a little early for this town," Clint said.

"What brings you here?" Bat asked, sitting down and turning his chair so he could see as much of the place as Clint could. He knew Clint would watch his back—in fact, he was one of the few men Bat would trust to do so—but that didn't make it any easier to actually sit with his back to the room.

"I was invited."

"By Witmer?"

"That's right."

"To watch and not play?"

"Right again."

"Why would you come?"

"It should be interesting," Clint said. "Besides, I thought I might see some people I know here."

"No doubt you will. Why didn't he ask you to play?"

"That's a long story."

Bat looked around the room.

"I think I've got time."

Clint told Bat the story, leaving out the part about Witmer not wanting to play against him. There was no point in tweaking Bat's ego. Instead he told Bat that he was invited so Witmer could hit him up for a partnership and have him handle security.

"A partnership with Witmer?"

"That's right."

"Why would you do that?" Bat asked. "The way I hear it, he's been living at the bottom of a bottle for a couple of years."

"You heard that, huh?"

"You didn't?"

"No."

"Is it true?"

"It's true," Clint said, "but he's got his life back on track now. In fact, he's looking to get married and settle down."

"I hope he's not depending on the money from this game for that."

"I'm afraid he is."

"Well, then, I hope you've got a lot of money stashed away to fix this place up with," Bat said, "because I intend to win this game."

"I knew that without being told."

"I've never understood why you're friends with him."

"I've never questioned your friendships."

Bat smiled.

"I'm not saying I question it," he said. "I'm just saying I've never understood it. Your friends are your friends. I'd never question you on that."

"Thanks."

"Why is he your friend, anyway?"

Clint smiled now.

"I like him."

"Why?"

Clint shrugged.

"Same reason I like you, I guess."

"And what's that?"

"I've never been able to figure that out either."

TEN

By dinnertime ten players had arrived. Witmer was sitting with Clint and Bat in the hotel dining room, having finally given in to the hunger pains in his stomach. Some of the other players were also in the room, eating. They had all either greeted Clint and Bat from across the room, or come over and said hello. There was no one present with whom Clint and Bat were particular friends.

"Doc Kennedy hasn't arrived yet," Witmer said.

"Kennedy?" Bat said. "I hope you didn't invite Holliday."

"I did," Witmer said, "but he's not coming."

"Who else is here?"

"Two of my dealers."

"Which dealer isn't here yet?" Clint asked.

"Jo."

"Jo Dillon?" Bat asked.

"That's right."

"Who else is here?" Bat asked. "Who else is coming? God, I haven't seen Jo in years."

Witmer reeled off some of the names of players who had already arrived.

"I know most of them," Bat said. "Witmer, you did good. This should be an interesting game."

"I tried to make it interesting," Witmer said. "I invited Holliday, and Ben Thompson, and Dick Clark, but they aren't coming."

"Who's coming who isn't here yet besides Kennedy?" Bat asked.

"Willie Tyler, Sam Veil, Bear Wilcox—"

"Bear?" Bat said. "I don't even know how he can hold cards in his hands without crushing them."

"He's a big man, all right," Clint said, frowning. If Bear got out of control, security would be harder than he thought.

Witmer finished his steak and pushed his chair back.

"I'm gonna go back outside."

As Witmer hurried from the room, Bat said, "He's a little excited about this, isn't he?"

"More than a little," Clint said. "He says the rest of his life depends on this game."

"On winning it?"

Clint nodded.

"Oh, no," Bat said, waving a hand.

"What?"

"You're not going to make me feel sorry for him," Bat said. "I'm not going to let him win. Besides, there are a lot of other people involved."

"You're the only one he's worried about."

"Flattery will not get you anywhere," Bat said. "I came here to win, even though I didn't know what kind of game it would be. Now at least I know it should be interesting, and there's probably more money in it than I thought.''

''I'm not asking you to let him win.''

''What are you asking me to do?''

''I haven't asked you to do anything.''

''Yet.''

Clint didn't respond.

''Is there a 'yet' at the end of that sentence?''

''No,'' Clint said, ''there's no 'yet' at the end of that sentence.''

''Good. Are you finished eating?''

''Yes.''

''Let's go to the saloon. That's where some of the other players might go later. Maybe we can get up a little side game.''

''The saloon is where the game is going to be held,'' Clint said. ''I don't know if it will still be open. They've got to set up.''

''Didn't you say you agreed to be partners with Witmer?'' Bat asked.

''Well, yes, for a while . . .''

''Then even if it's closed we can get in, can't we?'' Bat asked. ''After all, I'm with one of the bosses.''

ELEVEN

The saloon was still open for business. When Clint asked Culley, the man told him that they'd be open until two a.m., at which time they'd close and he'd set the place up for the game.

"That is," Culley added, "unless you want me to do something else?"

"No," Clint said. "If that's what you and Ken discussed, it's fine."

Clint and Bat claimed the table they had had before and sat with a beer in front of each of them. Before long players began to trickle in. They sat alone, or paired off, or sat in smaller groups. A short time later a game broke out at one table.

"I thought you wanted to play," Clint said.

"Not with them," Bat said. "See who that is?"

"Which one?"

"The pretty boy with the blond hair?"

"I see him."

"That's Eddie Pillman. He's a punk. I won't play in the same game as him."

"What if he's at your table tomorrow?"

Bat smiled.

"Then he won't be there for long, I can guarantee that."

"Who else do you know that I don't?"

"Probably a few," Bat said. "You haven't been playing much lately. See the fella with the black beard? Playing with Gilbert."

"I see him."

"He calls himself Count Eric Falcone. Claims to be some kind of Italian count."

"And is he?"

"Who knows? He's got a lot of money, though. That's what . . . counts."

Clint flinched and said, "Very funny."

Bat pointed out a few more players, and then Clint was able to point out one or two that he knew and Bat didn't.

"No friends," Bat said finally. "No Luke Short, no Dick Clark. Brett and Bart aren't here . . ."

"And I'm not playing," Clint said. "If you have no friends in the game, you'll have a better time of it."

"Why? I don't play any different with friends than I do otherwise."

"No?"

"No," Bat said, becoming indignant. "Name one time you saw me play differently."

"Never mind."

"Come on, name one."

"I can't."

"I try just as hard to beat you or Luke as I try to beat anyone—maybe even harder."

"You're right."

"Damn right I'm right."

Bat fumed for a few moments, then said, "Have you?"

"Have I what?"

"Ever played different with me?"

"I always give you my best, Bat," Clint said. "I know you'd never accept anything less."

"What about somebody else?" Bat asked. "Have you ever played different with anyone else?"

"Well . . . maybe once or twice, when I felt sorry for somebody. You know, I'd call a raise instead of raising myself when I felt sure I had the hand won."

"That's costing yourself money," Bat said. "You've done that?"

"Once or twice."

"Why?"

"Maybe it's because the game isn't about money for me like it is for you," Clint said. "Maybe I just like the game for the sake of the game."

"You'll never get rich that way."

"Well," Clint said, "maybe that's why I'm not rich."

"Maybe. . . ."

Eventually a game started at a table that involved some people Bat didn't mind playing with.

"You mind?" he asked Clint. "I see an open seat."

"No, go ahead," Clint said. "You've got to get yourself in shape for tomorrow."

"By the way," Bat said, "what time does the game start tomorrow?"

"Noon."

"That's good. If this place closes at two, that gives us plenty of time to play and still get some sleep."

"Good luck," Clint said. "I'll see you in the morning."

"Not going to stick around?"

"No," Clint said. "It's ten o'clock. I think I'll go to my room."

"I hope some more players show up between now and midnight," Bat said. "If this is all that's here, it should be some easy pickings. Interesting, but easy."

Clint watched as Bat walked over to the table, took out his wallet, and sat in the empty chair. Much as he might have liked to play, Clint thought he should maintain some distance from the players if he was going to be responsible for security.

He walked to the bar and said, "You need any help setting up later, Culley?"

"No, sir," Culley said. "I've done it before."

"I'll say good night, then."

"Good night."

Clint left the saloon and walked over to the hotel, where he found Ken Witmer still sitting out front.

"Two more hours," Witmer said.

"You going to sit here the whole time?"

"I guess so."

"Did Jo get here yet?"

"If she did," Witmer said, "I must have missed her."

"Well," Clint said, "she's not a player, she's a dealer. If she gets here late she'll still deal, right?"

"Right. I don't suppose you'd want to deal if she doesn't get here?"

"No," Clint said. "I think I'm wearing as many hats as I'd like to, Kenny. Thanks, anyway. Good night."

"Night, Clint."

Clint went inside and up the stairs to his room. When he got to his door he smelled something in the hallway, then he noticed that there was a light underneath his door. He hadn't left a light burning.

He tried the doorknob and found the door locked. He

used his key to unlock it, then opened it slowly and looked at the person on the bed.

"I was wondering when you'd get here. You're not surprised?"

"No."

"Why not?"

"I smelled your perfume out in the hallway."

She smiled.

"You still remember my perfume?"

"Your scent is hard to forget," he told her. He closed the door behind him and asked, "How are you, Jo?"

TWELVE

Jo Dillon looked older, but good.

"You've still got it, Jo."

She smiled.

"What makes you say that?"

"You got Witmer to lie."

"Oh, that," she said. "That wasn't hard."

She still had her jet-black hair, although it was streaked with some gray now. Her body looked a little thicker, but not in the least unattractive. Her face looked the same. Her mouth was wide, her cheekbones high. She had acquired a little bit of a double chin, but that, too, did nothing to detract from the fact that she was a handsome woman. Never a beauty in the true sense of the word, she still never had trouble turning male heads, and from what he could see, she still wouldn't.

"I've put on weight," she said, wriggling beneath his gaze.

"We all have."

"Not you," she said. "You look the same way you looked the last time I saw you."

"Which was . . ."

"Eight years ago."

"It couldn't be eight," he said.

"Oh, yes," she said, nodding. "I didn't have gray in my hair and sag in my breasts then."

"They don't look like they're sagging to me."

"How can you tell?" she asked. "I'm still dressed. In the old days you would have found me naked in your bed."

"Why not now?"

"I didn't know how you'd feel about having an old gal naked in your bed."

"I don't see a problem with it."

"Are you sure?" she asked. "It has been a long time, you know."

"Do you want me to help you?"

She stood up from the bed and said, "I might need help at that. I'm feeling fairly nervous right now."

"You?"

He walked up to her until they were almost touching.

"If you don't like what you see," she said, "don't tell me. Okay?"

"I've always liked what I saw when I looked at you, Jo," he said, "and I can't see that changing."

He took her in his arms and kissed her. Her scent was the same, and so was her kiss. She filled his arms more, but that had never been a complaint with him about a woman.

She muttered something and he said, "What?"

"Fifty," she said. "I'm fifty. I lie to some people about it, but not to you."

"You look ten years younger than that, easy," he said,

stretching the truth by maybe five. She did look marvelous for a fifty-year-old woman, and she felt just fine.

"Let's get those clothes off," he said, "so I can have me a real good look."

"Oh, God . . ."

She stood still while he undressed her. She'd been right about her breasts. Always full and heavy, they had some sag to them now, and her belly was not as flat as it used to be. When she was naked he stood back and regarded her gravely.

"Say something, damn you."

"I can't," he said. "I'm too stunned."

"You always were a good man with words," she said. "I've missed you, Clint."

"I've missed you, Jo."

"You know what?" she asked. "I don't even care if you're lying."

"I'm not."

"Well," she said, "get those clothes off so I can have a good look, too."

"And then we can stop talking."

She smiled and said, "That sounds good to me."

THIRTEEN

They made love slowly the first time, becoming reacquainted with each other's bodies. He'd forgotten how she loved to have her breasts kissed. Not just the nipples, but every part of her breasts. She shuddered when his lips brushed the heavy undersides, when he nipped the skin around the nipples, and then she moaned and grabbed him when he finally sucked a nipple into his mouth.

He'd also forgotten how good she was with her hands. She roamed all over his body, touching him in places no woman had touched him since the last time they were together. Clint had decided over the past few years that he preferred experienced women to young women, and Jo Dillon was a perfect example. She had a way about her that a young woman couldn't ever display.

When he was inside of her, she could do things with her muscles that made it hard for him to control himself. He slid his hands beneath her at one point to cup her ass and control their tempo, but she was still able to squeeze him with her muscles, almost driving him over the edge several times before he was ready.

And when he was finally ready, so was she. . . .

Later he kissed his way down over her belly, which she tried to cover with her hands.

"Stop," he said, swatting her hands away.

"It's too big," she protested. "I've gotten fat."

"No, you haven't." He kissed her belly. "You're just fine."

He delved further down, burrowing through the hair between her legs with his tongue until he could taste her. She jumped when his tongue touched her, and grabbed for his head. When his mouth became avid, she released his head and grabbed the sheet on either side of her.

"Oh, God," she cried out, "I'd forgotten how good you are at that!"

He grinned and lapped at her with his tongue while sliding one finger inside of her. She bit her lip to keep from screaming, and squirmed so hard that he had to pin her down with his elbows on her thighs to keep her from getting away from him.

"Oooh, oooh, oooooh . . ." she cried out as her body went taut and then seemed to explode. . . .

They lay together on the bed, his arm around her, as they caught up on the past eight years.

"You've been busy," she said. "I've been able to follow your activities when you showed up in the newspapers."

"I'm amazed we didn't see each other before now."

"When would you have had time for me?" she asked.

"What do you mean?"

"Oh, I've run into some of the women in your life over the past eight years."

"What?"

"Sure," she said. "Don't you think we meet each other and compare notes?"

"You're kidding."

"I'm not."

He looked down at her and saw that she was grinning.

"You are, aren't you?"

"No," she said, very pleased with herself. "That makes you uncomfortable, doesn't it?"

"Give me some names."

"Oh, no," she said. "We've all decided that we'll never tell you."

"But you have told me."

"But I didn't give you any names."

"Give me one."

She seemed to consider this.

"Come on," he said, "you can give me one."

"All right." She gave him a name.

"Where did you see her?"

"Seattle."

Clint had been to Seattle as recently as last year.

"When?"

She gave him a date and it was only a little after he'd been there.

"Too bad we didn't meet there," he said.

"Then you could have had both of us?"

"That sounds interesting."

She pinched the flesh on his side and said, "No, thank you. Being in bed with another woman is not something I find interesting."

"I do."

"Have you ever?"

"Have I ever what?"

"Been to bed with two women at one time?"

Clint hesitated, then said, "I don't know if I should answer that."

"You have, haven't you? You disgusting man."

"Why is it disgusting?"

She thought a moment then said, "Well, I guess from your viewpoint it wouldn't be. Who were you in bed with?"

"Don't you know?" he asked. "I mean, if you've run into some of the women I've been with, didn't any of them tell you?"

"The ones I've spoken to didn't say anything about a second woman in bed with you."

"Well, maybe they lied."

Abruptly she got to her knees and looked down at him. "Tell me what it's like."

"What what's like?"

"To be in bed with two women at one time," she said. "How do you know which one to pay attention to?"

"Jo—"

"When you're making love to one, what's the other one doing?"

"Jo—"

"Can you concentrate on both of them at one time?"

"Jo—" he said, grabbing her and pulling her to him.

"What?"

"Right now I only want to pay attention to one woman."

"Me?"

"Yes," he said, sliding his hand between her legs, "you . . ."

Later she said, "We can't do this once the game starts, you know."

"Why not?" he asked.

"Because I'm a dealer."

"But I'm not a player."

"But Ken is, and you're his partner."

"How do you know that?"

"He told me."

"And when did he tell you this?"

"A little while ago, when I got here."

"Are you sure he didn't tell you before that?"

"Like when?"

"Like when he asked you to come and deal?"

"Were you partners then?"

"No."

"Then how could he tell me?"

"Never mind," he said, "let's go to sleep. You've got a big day tomorrow."

Clint hoped that Jo was telling him the truth. If Witmer had told her ahead of time, it meant that he felt sure Clint would agree, and if there was anything Clint hated it was being predictable.

FOURTEEN

By morning Jo had gone back to her own room, which was on the same floor. When Clint went down to breakfast, many of the players were there, but there were no more than two people per table. Apparently, they had either paired up, or decided to eat alone after what had happened in the saloon last night—whatever that was. Bat was in a corner, eating alone, and Clint walked over and joined him.

"How did you do last night?"

"Can't you tell from the dirty looks I'm getting?" Bat asked.

Clint made a show of looking around.

"I don't see any dirty looks, but I guess you're telling me that you won."

"Of course."

The waiter came over and Clint ordered steak and eggs.

"How was your night?" Bat asked.

"Why do you ask?"

Bat looked at him.

"I'm just making conversation."

"Well . . . my night was fine. I slept very well, thank you."

"Fine. Have some coffee while you're waiting for your food. I had him bring an extra cup."

"Thanks." Clint poured his cup full. "Did you see Ken last night?"

"When I came back to the hotel he was gone," Bat said, "but it was after two. I guess everyone who was going to arrive by that time did."

Clint looked around the room and counted thirteen people.

"Are all these fellas players?"

"Far as I can tell, and there's more than this."

"Looks like Ken didn't have to worry."

"What was he worried about?"

"He thought that maybe no one would come."

"Why not? Wave money around and somebody will come. Oh, you mean because of his problem?"

Clint nodded.

"Well, you didn't know he was a drunk, did you?"

"No."

"Then I guess there are those who haven't heard about it," Bat said, "and those who have, but don't care."

"Good for him."

Clint's breakfast came and he dug in.

"I heard Jo got in last night," Bat said, "so I guess all the dealers are here and we're ready to go."

"Good. I want things to go smoothly for Ken."

Bat smiled and said, "I want things to go smoothly for me."

At that moment Ken Witmer entered the dining room and looked around at the players. Some of them looked up and waved to him, others ignored him in favor of their food. Finally he walked over to the table Clint was sharing with Bat.

"Do you mind if I join you?"

Clint looked at Bat, since he was the first one to claim the table.

"No, sit down," Bat said, pointing to a chair with his knife. "Looks like you've got a good turnout."

"Thank God," Witmer said. "Doc Kennedy was the last to arrive late last night."

"Doc's here," Bat said. "Good. How many others?"

"We'll have three tables of eight players," Witmer said.

"Five-card stud, huh?" Bat asked.

Witmer nodded.

"Once we pare down to less players we can mix the games if everyone wants."

"I'd rather stick to one game," Bat said. "Stud's as good as any."

"That's what most of the players will say, I think," Clint said.

The waiter started over, but Witmer waved him away.

"You're not eating?" Clint asked.

"I ate earlier," Witmer said.

"How do things look at the saloon?" Bat asked.

"Everything is ready."

"You going to be serving liquor during the game?"

"Sure, the bar will be open," Witmer said. "It's up to the players if they want to drink or not."

"Only a fool drinks and gambles," Bat said, "but that's who I make most of my money off of, fools. That's just what I did last night."

Clint looked around to see if anyone was listening. Obviously, somebody had played poker with Bat last night while drinking and had lost a lot of money. Apparently, the big loser either wasn't in the room or chose not to acknowledge that he was.

"How are you setting up the tables?" Bat asked.

"Drawing numbers," Witmer said. "Numbers one through eight will sit at one table, then nine through sixteen, and so on."

"I hope I get some decent players at my table."

"So do I," Witmer said.

Bat looked across the table at Witmer.

"It's kind of unusual, you know."

"What is?"

"For the person running the game to also play in it."

Witmer stared at Bat for a few moments.

"You think people will object?" Witmer looked truly concerned.

Bat and Clint exchanged a glance, and then Bat said, "Nah. You got as much right to play as anyone."

Witmer's shoulders seemed to relax as he breathed a sigh of relief.

"Well," he said, "I think I'll just go over to the saloon and wait."

"Can we come over anytime and draw a number?" Bat asked.

"Sure," Witmer said, "first one draws the first number, when they show up."

"I'll be over," Bat said. "Like to get some sense of where I'm going to sit as soon as possible."

Witmer nodded and stood up.

"See you over there."

Clint and Bat watched Witmer walk away.

"You scared him," Clint said.

"I was just funning with him," Bat said, "although it is unusual."

"I don't think anyone will object."

"No one is afraid enough of him to make an issue of it," Bat said.

"He's a pretty good poker player, Bat."

"Technically, maybe," Bat said, "but he's too emotional, he's got too much of an ego."

"Which you don't."

"Hell, no," Bat said, "I just know how good I am."

FIFTEEN

After breakfast Clint and Bat walked over to the saloon. The front doors were open, and when they walked in they saw that the place had been totally rearranged. All the tables were gone and there were three larger, round tables in the center of the room. On each table was a rack of chips and half a dozen decks of cards. The chips were white, red, blue, gray, and black.

Culley was behind the bar, and Witmer was in front of it. On the bar next to him was a bowl with slips of paper in it. On each slip was written a number from one to twenty-four. There was no one else in the room.

"Numbers," Witmer said, pointing to the bowl.

Bat and Clint approached the bar. Bat stuck his hand in and came out with a number. He opened the slip and showed it to Witmer.

"Number one," Witmer said, shocked.

Bat looked at Clint and said, "That's an omen if I ever saw one."

"I think you're right."

"It's worth a beer," Bat said.

"This early?" Clint asked.

"Just one," Bat said, "before the game."

"Okay."

"Culley," Witmer said, "three beers."

"Kenny," Clint said.

Witmer looked at him, then said to Culley, "Make that two beers."

Culley drew two and put them on the bar.

"I'll take mine to table one," Bat said. He picked it up and looked around. "Which one is table one?"

"That one." Witmer pointed.

Bat walked over and sat at the table with his beer. The tables were centered in the room, so there was no way he could sit with his back to a wall. He was going to have to depend on Clint to watch his back.

They heard footsteps on the boardwalk outside and turned to look at the door. A man walked in and looked around.

"Bat."

"Kendall," Bat said. "I don't believe you've met Clint Adams."

"Mr. Adams."

"Hello, Mr. Will."

Kendall Will walked forward and shook hands with Clint.

"Mr. Will," Witmer said. "Welcome to San Sebastian."

"Mr. Witmer." Will shook hands with him.

Kendall Will was tall and thin, almost painfully thin. His dark hair was slicked back and came to a widow's peak. He looked like a man who had just gotten over a long illness—except that he always looked like that. He was wearing a long duster and a big black hat. He was forty and looked fifty.

"Which table will I be at?"

"Table two."

"Ah," Will said. "And who will be dealing at table number one?"

"Jo Dillon."

Will raised an eyebrow, but he couldn't complain. Jo Dillon had been dealing poker for years.

"And table three?"

"Waco Muldoon."

Will looked at Witmer.

"Waco's a loose cannon," Will said. "Who's handling security?"

"I am," Clint said.

Will thought a moment, then nodded.

"Where can I leave my coat?"

"I'll take your coat," Clint said, "your hat . . . and your gun."

"My gun?"

"Your gun," Clint said. "House rule."

Will matched stares with Clint, then reached inside his coat, removed his gun belt, and handed it over. He followed with the coat and hat. Beneath the coat he wore a three-piece suit that had come from a tailor in New York.

"I'll see to the cards and chips," he said, and walked to his table.

Clint turned to Witmer and said, "Where?"

"My office, back there."

Clint walked to the back and through a door into Witmer's office. There was no desk and no furniture, and a lot of dust. He hung the coat on a coatrack in a corner and went back outside.

"I know," Witmer said, "it needs work. I'll get a desk soon."

"Sure."

Witmer looked at Bat sitting at table one, and Kendall Will sitting at table two, inspecting the seals on the decks of cards, and said, "Okay, it's started."

SIXTEEN

Everything went smoothly and by twelve-thirty all the players were seated. At table one with Bat were Doc Kennedy, Gentleman Jim Everett, Willie Tyler, Sam Veil, Tyler Duncan, Big Ben Haley, and Hiram Excess.

And Jo Dillon.

When Jo entered the saloon, she and Clint exchanged a glance.

"Good morning, gentlemen." She nodded in the direction of Kendall Will, who nodded back. The third dealer, Waco Muldoon, had also arrived. He was a big man with a bushy red beard, and he half rose and inclined his head toward Jo.

"Ken?" she said.

"Table one, Jo."

She nodded and walked to the table where Bat was sitting talking with Jim Everett and Sam Veil.

"Bat," she said.

"Hello, Jo. Do you know these gents?"

"I know Gentleman Jim."

"Miss Dillon."

"Jo, this is Sam Veil."

"Mr. Veil."

Clint came and took Jo's wrap, deposited it in the back room. When he came back out Jo was inspecting the seals on the cards.

Now, half an hour later, she was counting out the chips for each player's five-thousand-dollar buy-in, as were the other dealers.

Clint walked to the front door, closed it, and locked it. He turned, looked at Witmer, and smiled.

"We're ready to begin," Witmer said. He had drawn a number himself and had ended up at table two.

Everyone's guns were in the back room, and the door was locked. The key was in Clint's pocket. Clint walked over to the bar and exchanged a look with Culley.

"Anybody have anything to say?" Witmer asked.

Heads turned as players looked at each other, and most of them shook their heads.

"Let's get on with it," One-eyed Dugan said.

"Yeah," Eddie Pillman said. "We came here to play cards, didn't we?"

Witmer walked to his table and sat down.

"Deal."

Across the street Jesus Mendez and Tino Rosario watched as the front doors of the saloon closed.

"What is going on?" Rosario asked. "Who are all those men?"

"I do not know," Mendez said, "but we cannot do anything while Witmer is around them. We will just have to wait."

"Can we wait with the *putas*?" Rosario asked.

Mendez looked at him and said, "Yes, Tino, go and wait with the *putas*. I will come for you when the time is right."

Rosario walked away and Mendez made himself comfortable in the doorway of an abandoned store.

SEVENTEEN

For the most part Clint stayed out of the way. He watched the game from the bar, nursing a beer until it got warm, then trading it in for another until that one got warm, and so on.

Culley walked back and forth from the tables to the bar, taking drink orders. Clint noticed that everyone was drinking except for Bat, Doc Kennedy, Gentleman Jim Everett, Kendall Will, Witmer and Hiram Excess. Jo Dillon was drinking, but she was making a shot glass of whiskey last an hour.

In the first five hours one player from each table busted out of the game. One of them, Eddie Pillman, took it badly and Clint had to take him aside.

"You busted out of the game, Eddie," Clint said. "Time for you to leave, like the other players who busted out."

"B-but that feller, Dugan? He bluffed that last hand. I had the winning hand."

"Correction, you *folded* the winning hand."

"That wasn't fair."

"Eddie," Clint said, "take my advice. The next time you save up five thousand dollars, keep it."

"I want my gun."

"I'll have it brought to the hotel for you."

"Hey, I want my—"

"Let me walk you out, Eddie," Clint said. He clamped his hand on the man's elbow and led him to the door. The hold was so painful Eddie had no choice but to go along.

Clint unlocked the door and said, "Ask at the desk for your gun in the morning, Eddie . . . just before you leave town."

"But—"

Clint pushed him out and closed the door in his face.

Jesus Mendez watched as a man was pushed out of the saloon and the door was slammed in his face. Struck by an idea, he left his doorway and started to follow the man. It soon became clear that he was heading for the hotel. Mendez quickened his pace to catch up. The man heard him and turned, but Mendez had his gun out, even though he could see that the man was unarmed.

"Wha—"

"*Silencio.* In the alley, quickly."

He took a handful of Pillman's shirt and pulled him into the alley.

"What do you want?"

"I will ask the questions," Mendez said, putting the barrel of his gun beneath Pillman's chin.

"O-okay," Pillman said. "Okay. You ask the questions."

"What is going on in the saloon?"

"A poker game."

"A what?"

"Poker game," Pillman said. "You know, cards?"

"Poker?"

"Yeah, it's a big game," Pillman said, "lots of money involved."

Mendez hesitated, then said, "Money?"

"Yeah, yeah, lots of money."

"And how long will this game go on?"

"Maybe for days."

"And who is running this game?"

"Feller named Witmer, Ken Witmer."

"Witmer."

"Yeah, Witmer."

Mendez stood there, taking in the information.

"So . . . can I go?"

"How many men are in the saloon?"

"About twenty-three or -four, I think," Pillman said. "As men lose, though, they have to leave."

"So they will leave one by one?"

"Uh, yeah, sometimes more."

Again Mendez took time to take this in.

"So . . . can I go?"

Mendez holstered his gun, and Pillman turned to walk away. Before he could, though, Mendez pulled out a knife, reached around, and slit Pillman's throat. As the man gurgled and fell, Mendez caught him and dragged him further into the alley. When he left the alley he headed for the whorehouse. He had to talk to Rosario about this.

EIGHTEEN

A break was called at midnight and players stood up to stretch their legs. Most of them went to the bar for a drink. Clint walked over to table one, where Jo Dillon was tearing up the used deck. When the game started again she'd break the seal on a new deck.

"How's it going?" Clint asked.

She smiled and said, "Bat's ahead. What a surprise, huh?"

"Who else?"

"Gentleman Jim," she said. "Everybody else is losing, and Sam Veil is about to bust out of the game."

"Can I get you another drink?"

"No," she said, looking at her almost empty shot glass, "I can nurse this for another, oh, twenty minutes or so. It's just to keep my mouth wet . . . you know?"

He thought about her mouth being wet and shifted his feet.

"At this rate this could take a while," she said. "I thought there'd be more than three players missing by now."

"I guess things are pretty evenly matched."

"I think Bat and Jim should have this table in hand pretty soon. By tomorrow afternoon we'll probably be combining tables."

"And then you'll get a break."

"Right," she said, flexing her fingers. "My fingers are not as young as they used to be."

He thought about what her fingers had been doing the night before and lifted his legs again.

"Well," he said, "I'll just check with the other dealers."

"Sure."

He walked over to the second table while Kendall Will was standing and stretching his back.

"How's it going, Mr. Will?"

"Fine," he said. "Two players will bust out in the next half hour. By tomorrow afternoon I'll be down to four."

"Sounds like the game is moving along."

"The cream is starting to rise to the top," Will said. "Witmer's doing well."

Clint nodded and moved on to the third table, where Waco Muldoon was combing out his beard with his hands.

"Waco."

"Hello, Clint. Things are moving along."

"Anybody in a foul mood?"

"A couple of players are on the verge of busting out, but they'll take it okay. It's part of the game."

"That's good."

"Bear is having an incredible run of luck. I've never seen him win so much."

"Really?"

Muldoon, a big man himself, shook his head and said,

"I don't know how he doesn't just crush his cards in his hands."

"I don't either."

They shook their heads at each other and Clint moved away, to be intercepted by Witmer.

"It's going really well, Clint," he said. "My cards are really good."

"That's fine, Ken."

"How about the players who busted out?"

"Shouldn't be any trouble," Clint said. "Pillman was a little upset, so I didn't give him back his gun."

"That's good," Witmer said. "I knew I could count on you to keep the lid on things."

"I'm doing my best."

"How's Bat doing?"

"He and Jim are holding the first table."

"Too bad," Witmer said. "I thought maybe he'd have a run of bad luck and I wouldn't have to face him."

"Did you ever think that maybe *you'd* have the run of bad luck?"

"No, not me," Witmer said. "I can feel it, Clint. I'm very, very hot."

"Well," Clint said, "for your sake I hope you stay that way, Kenny. How much longer are you going to play tonight?"

"Probably about three hours, then we'll take a break so everyone can get some sleep."

"These dealers could probably have used some relief."

"I know that," Witmer said, "but I didn't have the money to hire six dealers, Clint."

"Well," Clint said, "they seem to be holding up pretty well."

"When we get down to two tables tomorrow they can start to alternate."

"Good."

"Who's winning at table three?"

"Looks like Bear."

"Really? Who would have thought?" Witmer checked his pocket watch. "Well, time to get started again."

He walked to table two and said, "Break's over, folks. Time to get back to work."

Some of the players left their unfinished drinks at the bar, while others brought them with them to the tables.

Clint went back to the empty bar, where Culley handed him a beer.

"Things look like they're goin' well," the big man said.

"So far."

"How's the boss doing?"

"He's winning."

"Do you think he's got a chance at this game, Clint?" Culley asked.

"If his cards are as good as he says they are," Clint said, "I don't see why not."

"I hope he does," Culley said. "I want to be in on this, you know?"

"Culley," Clint asked, "do you know why he thinks San Sebastian is going to grow?"

"No," Culley said, "he hasn't told me . . . but then I haven't asked."

"Why not?"

"It don't matter to me," the bartender said. "I've worked for him enough times to know that if he says it's gonna grow, it's gonna grow."

"You trust him that much?"

"He ain't never been wrong with me, Clint."

"Never?"

Culley grinned.

"Well, once, maybe."

Clint turned and looked at the tables, saw that the games were under way again.

''I'm going to take a look outside,'' Clint said, ''see if any of the losers are hanging around. Keep an eye on things, okay?''

''Sure.''

Clint walked to the front door, unlocked it with the key, and stepped outside.

NINETEEN

Mendez opened the door and saw Rosario's naked ass pumping up and down in bed. He knew it was his friend's butt because of the puckered scar where a dog had bitten him when they were children.

Beneath Rosario a woman moaned and cried out. Mendez could see her smooth, naked legs spread wide, and her arms around Rosario's back. Mendez hated to interrupt his friend.

At that moment Rosario saved him the trouble. Suddenly he was roaring and pounding into the woman, and Mendez knew he only had to wait a few seconds more and his friend would be finished.

Eventually Rosario rolled off the woman, laughing.

"*Ay, bonita*, you wait a little while and we will do it again, eh?"

"You do not have a little while," Mendez said.

Rosario looked up in surprise and laughed when he saw Mendez.

"Hey, Jesus," he called out, "you want to ride the *puta*, eh? She is a good one, amigo."

Mendez looked at the woman, who was staring back at him boldly. She had very large breasts and very red lips, although some of the red had been smeared by Rosario's kisses. Her hair was black, and was flying wildly about her head.

"We do not have time, Tino," Mendez said. "Get dressed."

"Is it time already?" Rosario complained. "I have only ridden the *puta* twice."

"That will have to be enough, *cabrón*. We have to talk. Get dressed. I will wait downstairs."

"Are you sure you want to wait downstairs?" the Mexican whore asked.

When he looked at her, she had hiked her hips up so he could see her crotch, and she was fingering herself.

"Get dressed," Mendez said. If this whore was the best this town had to offer, his dick was going to stay very dry and very limp.

It was dark outside, and quiet. It was unusual for most towns to be this quiet around midnight. Usually you heard voices laughing and talking and yelling, and music, sometimes even shots. It was quiet in San Sebastian at midnight . . . too quiet.

Clint walked back and forth in front of the saloon, and then checked the alleys on either side. It was beyond him why Witmer thought San Sebastian was going to grow. Was it that he wanted to believe it because Carmen was just across the border? Or did he know something?

Clint walked a little ways from the saloon in either direction, then headed back. The street was quiet, and the losers seemed to have gone to bed. He was going to go back inside when he thought he heard something. A moan of some kind. He turned around and looked into the darkness. He almost gave up when he heard it again, and then he saw the man staggering from two alleys down, obviously hurt.

He ran toward the man, who fell to the ground before he could reach him. When he got there he dropped to his knees and turned the man over. It was Eddie Pillman, and his throat had been cut. From the looks of the wound he should have been dead.

"Eddie? What happened?"

The injured man was only able to gurgle as blood poured from his mouth.

"Eddie—"

There was a rattle, and then the man was still. He *was* dead, and Clint wondered how he had been able to stagger from the alley with that wound—and, if it had happened shortly after he'd left the game, how he had managed to live this long.

Clint looked around but there was no one on the street to help him. He'd have to leave the body on the street and go back to the saloon for help. He hated to interrupt the game, but a man was dead—one of the players—and this could have a bearing on the game itself.

He headed back for the saloon, hoping that San Sebastian had a sheriff.

TWENTY

‘‘Goddamn it!’’ Ken Witmer said for the tenth time in an hour. ‘‘Why did this have to happen now?’’

‘‘I’m sure Eddie Pillman would be sorry he ruined your game,’’ Clint said, ‘‘if he was still alive to be sorry, that is.’’

They were in the saloon, standing at the bar. The other players were sitting at tables, but there were no games in progress and everyone was having a drink.

Clint had returned to the saloon and informed everyone what had happened. He’d asked Witmer if there was a sheriff in town, and he said he thought so.

‘‘You think so? You mean you don’t know?’’

‘‘I’ve never had occasion to talk to a sheriff,’’ Witmer said, ‘‘but I assume there is one.’’

‘‘Culley?’’

‘‘I don’t know, Clint.’’

‘‘Would you do me a favor and find out, please?’’

"Sure thing."

Culley left, the games stopped, everyone got their own drinks, and they were all waiting around to find out if San Sebastian had a sheriff.

Bat came over to where Clint was standing with Witmer.

"What do you think happened?" he asked.

"Who knows?" Clint asked. "I don't know if he was robbed, or what. I hate leaving him lying out in the street."

"We could have a few men go out and carry him in here," Bat suggested.

"In here?" Witmer asked.

"No," Clint said, not because Witmer was outraged, "I think we better leave him where he is. The sheriff—if there is one—can trace his steps back to where it happened. There's got to be a blood trail."

"*We* could do that," Bat said.

"I don't want to do that," Clint said. "It's not my responsibility."

"What if the town doesn't have a sheriff?" Bat asked. "Whose responsibility is it then?"

"Not Clint's," Witmer said. "He's security for the game, not the town."

"And Pillman's a player," Bat said.

"Pillman *was* a player," Witmer said. "Once he went out the door he wasn't a player anymore."

"He's in town because of the game," Bat argued. "I think that makes him our responsibility."

"Ours?" Clint asked.

Bat shrugged and said, "Well, I'm here to help."

"We may not need help," Witmer said. "If there's a sheriff we can let him take care of it, and we can go on with the game."

"Not tonight, I'm afraid," Clint said.

"I agree," Bat said. "Nobody feels like playing anymore tonight."

"Great," Witmer said, "just great. Goddamn it, why did this have to happen?"

For the eleventh time.

When Culley returned he had a man wearing a badge in tow.

"This is Sheriff Montoya."

"*Sí,*" the man said, "I am *el jefe*. What has happened?"

"Did you see the man sprawled in the street, Sheriff?" Clint asked.

"*Sí,*" the man said. "Is he drunk?"

"He's dead."

"Dead? *Madre de Dios.*" The sheriff looked to be barely five foot five, and looked more like a farmer than a lawman. "How did he die?"

"He was killed," Bat said.

"His throat's been cut," Clint added.

"*Madre de Dios,*" the sheriff said again. "How did that happen?"

"That's for you to find out, Sheriff," Witmer said, "not us."

"Me?"

"Can you do something about getting him off the street?" Clint asked.

"*Sí*, I can take care of that," the man said, "but how will I find out who killed him?"

"We don't know," Witmer said, cutting in before Clint or Bat could say a word. "We have a game to play here. We can't be looking for a killer. That's your job."

"*Sí,*" the sheriff said, "I have heard of your game, señor. Was this man a player?"

"He was—" Clint said.

"Was," Witmer said, cutting in, "but he left. He wasn't a player when he was killed."

"Do you want us to keep these men here, Sheriff?" Clint asked.

"I do not know—"

"We can all alibi each other," Bat said helpfully. "All of us were in this room when it happened."

"Who found him?" Montoya asked.

"I did," Clint said.

"Well," the man said, removing his hat and scratching his head, "I suppose they can all go to bed then. Señor, your name?"

"Clint Adams."

"And you found the body?"

"Yes."

"Then would you accompany me, please, and the rest can go back to their hotel."

"All right," Witmer called out, "you can all go to the hotel. Be back here at noon tomorrow and we'll continue."

He turned and looked at the sheriff.

"Is there any problem with that, Sheriff?"

"I cannot see one, señor."

"Great!"

All of the players and dealers filed out, first stopping at the door to the office to collect their hardware and clothing.

"See you later," Jo said to Clint. "I want to hear everything."

"Okay."

After everyone had left, Culley said to Clint and Witmer, "I'll lock up."

"Thanks, Culley," Clint said. "Sheriff? Shall we go and take a look at the body?"

"I suppose so," the man said wearily.

"Not me," Witmer said. "I don't want to see any bodies

with slit throats. I'll go back to my room, Clint, and see you in the morning."

"All right, Witmer."

The disgruntled man went out of the saloon just ahead of them, mumbling, "God*damn* it, why did this have to happen now?"

TWENTY-ONE

When they reached the body, Sheriff Montoya looked down at it sadly. Clint couldn't tell if the lawman was sad for the dead man, or for himself for having to deal with it.

The sheriff leaned over the body briefly, as if to satisfy himself that the man was truly dead, then stood up.

"He is very dead."

"Yes, he is," Clint said. "I think he came out of that alley over there." He pointed.

"There is a trail of blood," Montoya said, and he and Clint followed it to the alley.

"It is too dark," Montoya said, at the mouth of the alley. "I will take a look when the sun comes up."

"Meantime," Clint said, "maybe you should see about getting the body off the street."

"Yes," Montoya said, "I will do that." He looked at Clint. "I know of you, señor. I am not ashamed to admit that you are probably more experienced in these matters than I am."

Clint admired the man for making that statement, but he didn't like what it implied.

"Any suggestions you have would be appreciated."

"All right," Clint said. "Get the body off the street and I'll join you in the morning to look in the alley. Is nine a.m. all right?"

Montoya swallowed, since his night's sleep had already been interrupted, but said, "Yes, that would be fine."

"All right," Clint said. "I'll leave you now, and see you tomorrow."

"*Gracias,* señor."

Clint left the sheriff heading back toward the body as he himself walked toward his hotel. When he got there Witmer was waiting out front.

"Well?"

"Well what?"

"Is he going to try to stop the game?"

"I doubt it."

"What did he say?"

"He said that I knew more about these things than he did," Clint said. "He asked me for suggestions."

"That's great," Witmer said. "That means the game can go on."

"Your grief over the death of one of your guests is touching, Kenny."

"Oh, come on, Clint," Witmer said. "I'm sorry Pillman's dead, but this is my life here, and we know that the killer is not one of the players."

"Maybe not one of the players who is still in the game," Clint said. "What about the others who busted out?"

"There were only two more, and what could they have against Pillman?"

"I don't know," Clint said, "but I'll suggest to the sheriff that he ask them."

"That's fine," Witmer said. "That won't interfere with the game either."

"I'm going to bed," Clint said. "I've got to meet the sheriff at nine."

He started into the lobby, then stopped and turned to face Witmer.

"If you're going to live here in San Sebastian, Kenny, and run a business, it might be wise for you to cooperate a little more with the sheriff."

"Yeah," Witmer said, "yeah, you're probably right, Clint. Okay, I'll be down here at nine a.m., too."

"Good idea," Clint said. "See you then."

As Clint entered the hotel, Witmer heaved a sigh of relief. Even more than he had anticipated, having Clint here was coming in handy.

When Clint reached his room he once again smelled Jo's perfume. The smell was too strong for her not to be inside the room. He opened the door and saw her naked form outlined beneath his sheet.

She sat up as he entered, and the sheet fell away from her breasts.

"Are you all right?"

"I'm fine," he said, "which is more than I can say for Pillman."

"It's too bad about him," she said. "What did the sheriff have to say?"

Clint gave her the same explanation he had given Witmer.

"If you have to meet him at nine you better come to bed and get some sleep."

"I intended to," he said. "I didn't expect to find you here."

"I know," she said, smiling. "I'm breaking my rule because of the unusual circumstances."

He stripped down to his shorts and got into bed with her. She snuggled up against him.

"I'll keep you warm."

Hot, was more like it, since her skin was like fire. He felt his body responding to her touch, and she became aware of it, too. She slid her hand down over his belly into his shorts and took hold of him.

"Seems like there's a part of you that isn't quite ready to go to sleep."

"I guess so."

"Well," she said, "we'll have to see if we can't tire him out."

She tossed the sheet off of them and slid his shorts down to his ankles and tossed them away. She slid her hands up his thighs and settled on her belly between his legs. She took his penis in her hand and pumped it up and down a few times until the head was bulging, then leaned over and ran her tongue around it.

"Mmmm," she said, licking him, and then opening her mouth and taking him inside. She slid her mouth up and down him a few times, wetting him thoroughly, and then began to suck.

He looked down at her between his legs, sucking him deeper and deeper. At times she would let him slide free of her lips and pump her fist, or rub her nose against the tip of him, or her tongue, and then she'd take him back in her mouth and suck him deeply again. She did all of this while keeping her eyes on him, which he found extremely erotic.

Finally, she slid her hand beneath him to cup his balls, and touched her finger to the spot just behind them while she continued to suck avidly. She moved her finger further back until it touched his anus, which she then probed, and suddenly he was crying out and spurting into her mouth.

She snuggled up against him again, covering them with the sheet, and asked, ''Tired?''

''Mmm-hmm,'' he said. ''Thank you kindly, ma'am. I think that did the trick.''

And it did. In moments, they were both asleep.

TWENTY-TWO

In the daylight the blood trail was easy to follow to the back of the alley.

"Look there," Clint said, pointing to deep groove marks in the dirt.

"What is it?" the sheriff asked.

"This is where the killer slit his throat," Clint said, "and then dragged him to the back of the alley. Those marks were made by his boot heels."

"Ah, I see."

Ken Witmer was there, but he was keeping quiet. He didn't know anything about these things, but he was hoping that his presence would work to his advantage with the sheriff.

"Can you tell anything else?" the sheriff asked Clint.

"From the tracks it looks like one man did this. Probably got the drop on Pillman because I wouldn't give him back his gun."

''Don't feel guilty about *that*,'' Witmer said.

''Don't worry,'' Clint said. ''I don't.''

Montoya scratched his head, and Clint knew he was at a total loss as to what to do next.

''Sheriff, there were two other players who left the game early,'' he said. ''Perhaps you should talk to them, find out where they were.''

''An excellent idea, señor.''

Clint gave him the other two players' names, and when they left the alley they went their separate ways.

''I've got to get over to the saloon,'' Witmer said. ''Will you be there today?''

''Where else would I be?''

''I thought you might be helping the sheriff try to find out who killed Pillman.''

''That's not my job, Kenny.''

''I'm glad to hear you say that.''

''I just thought of something, though.''

''What?''

''Remember those two strangers who rode into town the day before yesterday?''

''Lots of strangers rode into town the day before yesterday.''

''The Mexicans, the ones who weren't here for the game.''

''Okay, now I remember them. What about them?''

''I wonder where they are, and what they're here for, that's all.''

''Why don't you let the sheriff worry about that?''

''You're right,'' Clint said. ''I'll have to let him know.''

''What are you going to do now?''

''I just had some coffee this morning before meeting the sheriff,'' Clint said. ''I'm going to go and have a real breakfast.''

"All right," Witmer said, "I'll see you at the game."

"I'll be there."

The two men parted company, Witmer going to the saloon and Clint to the hotel.

Watching from across the street were Jesus Mendez and Tino Rosario. Rosario was still thinking about the whore he'd been with last night. He wanted to get back to her.

"Why don't we kill him now and get it over with?" he asked impatiently.

"Because it is daylight, and they found the man I killed last night."

"Why did you kill that man?" Rosario asked. "We were not supposed to kill anyone else, were we?"

"He saw me," Mendez answered, and left it at that. Rosario was not interested enough to pursue it.

"The *patrón* will be wondering what is taking so long," he said instead.

"He knows that killing a man is not an easy thing."

"It is not?"

"No, it is not," Mendez said. "You must find the right time and place to do it."

"Ah," Rosario said, "finding the time and place is not easy. I find killing a man *very* easy."

"I know you do, Tino," Mendez said, "but for now why don't you go back to your whores?"

"Now?"

"Now."

"*Bueno.*"

Mendez watched his friend walk off, wondering if and when his dick would fall off from fucking some rancid whore. Mendez had too much respect for his own dick to dip it into one of those women.

He watched as Ken Witmer walked to the saloon and

entered. He wondered what the *patrón*'s daughter saw in the gringo when she could have a real Mexican man, like himself. Aye, the *patrón*'s daughter, Carmen, now there was a woman. Smooth, dark skin, black hair, red lips, big breasts, long legs—a man would have to die and go to heaven to find another woman like that.

When Witmer disappeared inside the saloon, Mendez stepped out of his doorway and moved to one that was across from the saloon. He was having other thoughts this morning, as well, thoughts about money. The man he had killed yesterday had said there was a lot of money in this poker game. Mendez wondered if Don Carlos would mind if he and Tino stopped and picked up the money while they were killing the gringo.

Of course, there were a *lot* of gringos in the game, but all they had to do was wait and see who the winner was, and then take the money from him.

Mendez would have to think this over very carefully. He was determined to kill the gringo because he had told Don Carlos he would, and he was a man of his word. But when that was done, and they had taken the money, would there be any reason to even go back to Don Carlos's rancho? They would not have to work for him if they were rich.

Yes, he would definitely have to give this some more thought.

TWENTY-THREE

When Clint entered the dining room there were about half a dozen players there also eating. In the corner, sitting by herself, was Jo Dillon. Clint walked past the other tables, acknowledging the men with a nod, and sat down with her.

"I don't know how you get out of bed without waking me," she said.

"I move like a cat," he said.

She closed her eyes, shivered, and said, "Oooh, I know."

Clint waved a waiter over and ordered steak and eggs.

"Did you talk to the sheriff?" Jo asked.

"Yes, I did. He doesn't have the first idea what to do to find a killer."

"And you do?"

"I have a couple of ideas, yeah," Clint said, "but I don't really want to get involved."

"What if somebody else from the game gets killed?" Jo asked.

"What? Why should somebody else get killed?"

She shrugged.

"I don't know. Why was Pillman killed?"

"I don't know."

"Maybe somebody is after players in the game."

"Who were the other two players who busted out of the game early?" Clint asked.

She thought a moment, then said, "Ralph Benes and Hoby James."

"And where are they?"

"I don't know."

"The sheriff is supposed to talk to them," Clint said. "I wonder if they left town."

"Or if they're dead."

"I better check with the desk."

He got up, went out to the lobby, and asked the desk if Benes or James had checked out. They had not.

"Well?" she asked when he returned.

"They haven't left."

"I hope they're still alive."

"Jo, you're looking for trouble."

"I'm just thinking out loud, Clint. If another player gets killed—or worse, a dealer—would you get involved then?"

"I'd have to."

"Then why not do it now, before it can happen?"

He frowned at her as the waiter put his breakfast in front of him.

"You said you had some ideas," she said.

"I do." He told her about the two strangers who had ridden into town two days ago. "I haven't seen them since."

"Maybe you should find out where they are and talk to them."

Sourly, he said, "Yeah, maybe I should."

"Of course," she said, "maybe you shouldn't be listening to me at all."

"Yeah," he said, "maybe I shouldn't."

After breakfast Clint left the hotel and went looking for the boardinghouse. On the way he crossed paths with the sheriff, who was on his way to the hotel.

"Señor, where are you going?"

"I'm trying to find the boardinghouse in town."

"It is at the other end of town, a big building with two floors. It is run by a man named Sanchez." Montoya made a face. "A very disagreeable man."

"What makes him so disagreeable?"

"Mrs. Sanchez. I was hoping you would come to the hotel with me to talk to the other two men who left the game early."

"I have some other things to do, Sheriff, before the game starts. I'm sure you can handle them."

"*Sí*, I am sure I can, too," Montoya said, not sure at all.

"Let me know what happens."

"I will, señor."

Clint continued in the direction the sheriff had pointed him and eventually came to the two-story boardinghouse. He knocked on the door. It was answered by a man who looked as if he weighed three hundred pounds, although he was no taller than Clint. He was sloppy fat, and Clint could smell his sweat.

"Mr. Sanchez?"

"Yes, I am Jaime Sanchez. Do you want a room?"

"No," Clint said, "I wanted to ask you about two of your guests."

Sanchez laughed, and then launched into a coughing fit which Clint had to wait out before continuing.

"What's so funny?" he asked.

"I only *have* two guests."

"The two men who arrived the day before yesterday?"

"*Sí,*" Sanchez looked concerned. "You are not going to kill them, are you?"

"What makes you say that?"

"You look like a man who can kill people," he said, "and they look like two men somebody would kill."

"Do you know where they are?"

"I do not know for sure, but I can guess where one of them is. The first thing he asked me about was the whorehouse, and I am sure he spends more time there than he does here."

"Where is the whorehouse?"

"On the other side of town."

"Who runs it?"

"A very disagreeable woman."

"What makes her so disagreeable?" Clint asked.

The rumbling laugh came again, almost causing another coughing fit, and then Sanchez said, "Probably being married to me."

TWENTY-FOUR

Clint didn't have time to stop at the whorehouse now. He had to get back to the saloon for the game. He wanted to be there when the players began arriving again.

He had to pass the livery stable on the way back and saw a man he recognized leading his horse out. It was Ralph Benes, one of the men who had busted out of the game early.

"Benes!"

The man's head swiveled around as he heard his name.

"Oh, Adams," he said as Clint approached. "You startled me."

"Did the sheriff talk to you?"

"Just a short while ago," Benes said. "He said I could leave."

Benes looked completely calm and at ease, not at all like a man who was lying, so Clint chose to believe him.

"He was talking to Hoby when I left the hotel."

"Is James going to leave town today, too?"

Benes nodded.

"That's what he said. Just as soon as the sheriff is through with him."

"Did either of you know Pillman when you came here?"

"That's what the sheriff asked. Naw, we both met him here."

"What did you think of him?"

Benes laughed.

"He was probably the only poker player here who was worse than me."

"What about personally?"

"I didn't have an opinion of him personally," Benes said, "and I didn't have any reason to kill him, if that's your next question."

"It was."

"Why are you so interested?"

"He was a player," Clint said, "and somebody killed him. That makes me interested."

"You think somebody's gonna start targeting players to get killed?"

"I hope not."

"Sounds to me like a good time to leave this town."

"I won't keep you, then. Watch your back."

"Same to you."

Clint watched the man ride off and wondered if he was putting too much thought into what Jo Dillon had said. After all, she *was* only thinking out loud. What could someone have against a group of men who had gathered here from all over the country to play poker?

As he entered the saloon he saw that Culley, Witmer, and Bat Masterson were the only ones present. He checked the time and saw that it was 11:45.

"You don't think the killing yesterday scared everybody away, do you?" Witmer asked him.

"No, I don't, Kenny. They'll be here."

"Hell," Bat said, "if they don't show up it'll be me against you, Witmer."

Witmer looked over at Bat as if that concept frightened him. Clint wondered why Witmer had invited Bat. Why hadn't he just invited a bunch of players he knew he could beat if the money meant so much to him? Maybe there was more than just the money at stake here.

Maybe there was some pride, too.

"You got any coffee, Culley?" Clint asked.

"Comin' up, Clint."

At that point they heard footsteps and the players began to arrive. Clint was surprised that so many of them were arriving at the same time. When they entered but didn't sit down, he knew they had something on their minds.

"We got something we want to talk about," Doc Kennedy said.

Apparently, he'd been chosen spokesperson.

Witmer, unsure of himself, looked at Clint, but stepped forward and asked, "What's on your mind, Doc?"

"In light of what happened yesterday to Eddie Pillman," Kennedy said, "we want to keep our guns during the game."

Now Witmer did look to Clint and deferred.

"No guns," Clint said bluntly.

"Now listen, Adams—"

"You listen, Doc," Clint said. "No matter what happened out there, there's no need for guns in here."

"We'd feel safer with them," Kennedy said.

"And I'd feel safer if you didn't have them," Clint said. "I'll tell you what I will do, though. I'll let Bat keep his gun. If anything happens, he and I should be able to handle it.'' Clint turned and asked, ''Is that all right with you, Bat?''

Bat, who was making a show of playing solitaire, answered without looking up.

''It's fine with me, Clint.''

''What about you boys?'' Clint asked. ''You trust me and Bat?''

The players looked at each other and began to nod and reply that they did. All but Doc Kennedy, who was still looking stubborn.

''What if I don't want to give up my gun, Adams?'' he demanded.

''Then you don't play, Doc,'' Clint said.

''And you don't get your money back,'' Bat added.

Not wanting to be left out, Witmer said, ''That's right.''

''Now what's it going to be, Doc?'' Clint asked. ''Are you playing for the pot, or not?''

Kennedy took his time deciding, but finally undid his gun belt.

''I'm playing,'' he said, holding the belt out to Clint.

''Then let's get to it,'' Witmer said.

Culley helped Clint collect everyone's guns but Bat's and put them in the back room. While the players were getting to their tables and the dealers were cracking fresh decks, the door opened and Sheriff Montoya walked in.

''Señor?'' he called, waving at Clint.

''Don't let him cancel the game,'' Witmer said to Clint quickly.

''He's not going to cancel anything, Kenny, don't worry.''

Clint walked over to the sheriff, who beckoned him to join him outside.

''I talked to the other two players, señor, but they seemed sincere that they did not kill Señor Pillman.''

"I know," Clint said. "I talked with one of them before he left town."

"Alas, I do not know what to do next."

"Sheriff, two strangers rode into town the day before yesterday who are not involved in the game."

"*Es verdad?* This is true? Who are they?"

"I don't know," Clint said. "They were Mexican, and they're staying at the boardinghouse that your friend Sanchez runs."

"He is not my friend, señor," Montoya said, making a face. "A disagreeable man . . . and fat . . . and he stinks."

"Well, he said that one of these men is spending a lot of time at the whorehouse."

"Run by his fat and disagreeable wife."

"Yes. Maybe you should talk to these strangers, Sheriff. You know, just to find out what they want in San Sebastian."

"*Sí*, señor," Montoya said. "That would seem to be sound advice. I will do it."

"Very good."

"Again, thank you for your help, Señor Adams."

As the lawman hurried away, Clint thought that he had never received so much gratitude from a town sheriff before. It was almost disconcerting.

Clint looked up and down the street a few times before stepping back into the saloon. As he started to close the door, he thought he noticed something across the street. He paused but didn't see it again. Was it just his imagination?

Behind him he heard the sounds of chips, and men making their bets, and knew that the game was once again under way. He closed and locked the door, turned, and walked back to the bar.

TWENTY-FIVE

The activity in the game escalated. Part of the reason for that was that it was day two and players were starting to feel confident. For some of them it was a false confidence, and by five that afternoon six players had busted out of the game. That left fifteen of the original twenty-four players. They took a break at 5:10 to close down one of the tables, and for the dealers to arrange their schedule now that there would be three of them and only two tables.

During the break Witmer came over to Clint.

"It's going great," he said. "I'm doing really well."

"That's good, Kenny."

"And I'm still not at Bat's table. He's playing against Doc Kennedy and Bear now."

"Uh-huh."

"Do you think one of them can get him out of the game?"

"Doc's a good player," Clint said, "but I don't think Bear has a chance."

"That's what I was thinking."

"Why don't you want to play Bat, Kenny?"

"I thought that'd be obvious, Clint," Witmer said. "He's too good."

"Then why did you invite him?"

"You really want to know?"

"I wouldn't ask unless I did."

"I thought somebody else might take him out of the game," Witmer said, "you know, if he hit a cold streak at the right time? Then I thought I'd win. Word would get around that I won a game that Bat was in."

"Without ever having to sit at the table with him."

"Right."

"I don't think that's going to happen, Kenny."

"I guess not."

"It looks to me like you're going to have to sit down with him and Doc and a couple of the other good players before too long."

"I know," Witmer said. "There was a time, Clint, when I would have been excited about that—excited and confident."

"You'll get your confidence back, Kenny," Clint said. "It's just a matter of time."

"I guess so. Well, let's get started again."

He stepped up, called a halt to the break, and now the players went back to the two tables.

The odd dealer out at the beginning was Jo, and she came over to stand with Clint.

"Can I have a drink, please?" she asked Culley.

"Sure thing, ma'am."

"Bat's doing real well, Clint," she said.

"That's no surprise."

"No, but the fact that Bear is still in the game is. Have you watched him play?"

"Not much."

"Me neither. Has he gotten better?"

"Maybe."

"I guess I'll find out when I deal. How's your friend Witmer doing?"

"He's doing okay."

"He doesn't seem real confident."

He decided to tell her the truth.

"He's not, but maybe he'll get more confident as they go along."

"I've seen poker players lose their confidence before, Clint."

"And have you seen it come back?"

"In some cases yes," she said, "but in most cases no."

She turned to accept her drink from Culley.

"It's been my experience that when players lose their confidence it's hard for them to get it back for big money games. Saloon games, yes, but not the big money matches like this—or the bigger ones, like Denver and San Francisco."

"Well, I don't know what will happen with Kenny," Clint said. "I guess we'll just have to wait and see."

"You think anyone would mind if I sat down?"

"No, go ahead."

They had taken the third table and stuck it in a corner. She walked over and sat down to nurse her drink and wait her turn to deal again.

With only two tables going, Clint was able to watch more of the action. As the hours wore on he determined that Bear Wilcox's game had not improved all that much. The big man was just having an incredible run of cards. Clint had seen a good run like that carry a man right through a game, and he had seen it abandon a man just at the wrong moment. It would be interesting to see how it progressed with Bear.

At table one he noticed that Bat and Doc were taking in most of the money. He began to see even now that the fifteen remaining players would probably come down to Bat, Bear, Doc, and Kenny Witmer at the end, unless somebody's luck suddenly took a turn for the better or the worse.

He walked to the front of the saloon and looked out the window. He wondered how Sheriff Montoya was doing trying to track down those two strangers.

He peered across the street and now he was sure he saw something. It looked as if someone was standing in a doorway. The killer? Or just somebody curious about the game? Or worse, somebody looking to rob the game?

There was no point in going across now to find out. He'd probably just scare him away. Sometime in the near future, though, he'd find out who he was and what he wanted. For now he'd let the man think he had gone unseen.

He turned and went back to watch the game.

TWENTY-SIX

Rosario was riding his favorite whore when there was a knock on the door. He stopped, because Mendez would not have knocked.

"*Qué pasa?*"

"I would like to talk to you," a voice said. "I am Sheriff Montoya."

"The sheriff," the whore said. "What have you done?"

Rosario smiled at her.

"Nothing, my beauty. He says he only wants to talk. Let him in, eh?"

"*Sí.*"

He slid his softening penis out of her, and she stood up and reached for her robe.

"No, no," Rosario said, "I want to see you naked."

"Oh, you . . ." she said, and padded naked to the door, giggling.

Rosario took that moment to hide his loins beneath the bedsheet, as well as a knife and his gun.

The whore—whose name was Aurora—opened the door and stepped back to give the sheriff a good look.

Montoya's eyes popped as he saw her big, naked breasts, and—since he was short and she was tall—they were almost in his face.

"Sheriff Montoya," Rosario said, "come in, come in."

Montoya shuffled into the room.

"What can I do for you?" Rosario asked. He would have preferred that Mendez was here to talk to the lawman, but since he wasn't he was going to have to brazen it out. He knew he wasn't going to be able to shoot the lawman—not here anyway. It would attract too much attention. If he was going to make a move against the man it would have to be with his knife, and for that the sheriff would have to come closer.

"I have some questions for you, señor," Montoya said, unable to take his eyes off of Aurora's huge tits and brown nipples. Montoya's own wife had grown fat over the years, and her breasts sagged badly. He did not frequent the whorehouse in town—his wife would kill him—and so had not seen a pair of breasts like this in many years.

"Tell me what you wish, Sheriff," Rosario said expansively, "and I will try to help you."

By the time it got dark there were six players left, and they were all at one table. Someone had suggested upping the limits, and players had started falling from the game fast.

Now, with the six players left, it had developed into a fine game, one that was fun to watch.

The six players were: Bat Masterson, Ken Witmer, Bear

Wilcox, Doc Kennedy, Gentleman Jim, and Hiram Excess—who had made a miraculous recovery from a point where he was one hand from being out of the game.

The surprising thing was that four of these six players—Bat, Doc, Gentleman Jim, and Excess—had been at table one the whole time. At one point it had looked as if Bat and Doc Kennedy had the table wrapped up, but Gentleman Jim had come back gradually, while Hiram Excess had made a startling recovery by taking three straight big pots.

"Gentlemen," Ken Witmer said, "I think it's time for a break."

"Jo!" Kendall Will called.

"My deal," she called back from her corner table.

Will stood up and stretched his back. Waco had gone for a nap in the back room.

The players also stood up and began to stretch and mill about, eventually finding their way to the bar.

Clint found himself standing with Bat.

"It's developed into an interesting game," Bat said.

"I've noticed."

"Your friend is playing well."

"Well enough?"

"Maybe," Bat said, accepting a beer from Culley. "Bear's luck has run out. He'll be out of the game within the next three hands."

"Who else?"

"Surprisingly enough, I think Gentleman Jim has about had it."

"And Excess?"

Bat shook his head.

"Jesus, I thought he was gone hours ago. He keeps hanging on."

"And Doc?"

''Doc's tough,'' Bat said. ''I think it's going to come down to me, Doc, and Witmer.''

''That *should* be interesting,'' Clint said. ''Think it'll happen tonight?''

''That I don't know,'' Bat said. ''Bear should be out, but the other five of us might have to come back at noon tomorrow.''

Clint thought about the figure in the doorway across the street. He told Bat about it.

''You want me to help you take a look later?''

''No,'' Clint said. ''We'll just stumble around in the dark. It can wait.''

''Okay,'' Bat said, ''but just say the word and we'll check it out.''

''Break's over,'' Witmer said. ''Let's get back to work.''

TWENTY-SEVEN

By three a.m. there were still five players in the game. Bear Wilcox had dropped out about one a.m., and Clint had asked him to stay around.

"What for?" Bear asked.

"I might need some help, Bear."

"Why not?" the big man said. "I might as well see who wins."

"You did really well," Clint said. "You want a drink? On the house?"

Bear had a drink and Clint went and got him his gun. Two hours later they were still standing at the bar, watching the game.

"I think we're gonna have to call it a night," Witmer finally said. "I can hardly see."

"I could use some sleep, too," Gentleman Jim said. "I don't want to win badly enough to ruin my face."

"How are you gonna ruin your face?" Doc Kennedy asked.

"Bags, Doc," Gentleman Jim said, touching himself just below his eyes. "I need my beauty sleep."

"I don't need no beauty sleep," Hiram Excess said. "I just need some plain old sleep."

Excess was a remarkably homely man, but no one com mented on it—ever, because he was sensitive about it.

"Gentlemen," Clint said as the players were getting ready to leave, "if you don't mind I think it would be a good idea if we all walked back to the hotel together."

"I don't need a nursemaid," Excess said.

"None of us do, Hiram," Clint said. "I just think it's a good idea, if no one minds."

"I don't mind," Bat said, and since he didn't mind no one else took exception either.

The five players, Clint, and Bear Wilcox left the saloon together with the three dealers, Kendall Will, Waco Muldoon, and Jo Dillon. Culley stayed because he had a room right upstairs.

"You think somebody's gonna try to kill one of us, like Pillman?" Hiram Excess asked Clint.

"I just don't want anybody to get any ideas, Hiram," Clint said. "By this point in the game you're all carrying a lot of money. Why take any chances?"

"What kind of fool would even think about robbing this game?" Ken Witmer asked.

"There are lots of different kinds of fools in the world, Kenny," Clint said. "I don't know what the chances are that some of them are right here in town."

"Nobody's in San Sebastian," Witmer said.

"We are," Clint said.

And those two strangers, he thought. He wondered what

had happened between them and the sheriff, if anything. Was it possible that someone had heard about the game and gotten to town even earlier? Or how about the possibility that somebody simply had something against Eddie Pillman, and his death had nothing to do with the game?

That would be a coincidence, and that was the one thing Clint Adams had no belief in.

Across the street Jesus Mendez counted nine men and one woman.

''The odds are getting better,'' he told Tino Rosario, who was wishing he was still in a warm bed with a warm whore. ''Soon, most of the money will lie in the pockets of one or two—perhaps even the pocket of Ken Witmer.''

''Then we can kill him and leave,'' Rosario said.

''That's right.''

''And what do we do with the money?'' Rosario asked. ''Give it to the *patrón*?''

''That is a stupid question,'' Mendez said. ''We will kill Witmer because we told Don Carlos we would, but after that we are on our own.''

''We can keep the money?''

''That's right.''

''But Don Carlos—''

''As long as Ken Witmer is dead, Don Carlos won't care what we do, Tino. We have only to wait for this poker game to get down to the last two players.''

''And hope one of them is the gringo Witmer.''

''Right.''

''And if it is not?''

Mendez shrugged.

''We will still find a way to kill him and take the money.''

• • •

In the lobby of the hotel the men split up and went to their own rooms.

"Going to your room?" Clint asked Jo.

She nodded.

"We're too deep into the game for me to go to yours," she said. "You understand. You and Ken Witmer are partners. It wouldn't look right."

"I understand."

He watched from the lobby as she went up the stairs, then turned to find Bat watching him.

"Ready?" he asked.

"I'm ready," Bat said. "Let's go and see what your friend wants."

As they went out the door, Bat said, "I saw two as we were leaving the saloon."

"So did I."

"Recognize them?"

"Not in the dark."

"They'll probably be gone by the time we get there."

"If they are," Clint said, "we'll get them tomorrow. I think they'll stick around to see who wins the game."

"So you're convinced they're here because of the game?" Bat asked.

Clint nodded.

"Men like that can smell money," Clint said.

"Why not just rob the game?"

"Like Witmer said," Clint replied, "who'd want to rob this game with you and me and Doc Kennedy and some of the others around?"

"Yeah, but what if these fellas don't even recognize us?"

"They'll still wait for the numbers to be in their favor, don't you think?"

"That's what you and I would do," Bat said. "Who can

know what these fellas will do? We don't even know who they are."

"We will," Clint said, "soon enough."

Clint and Bat approached the area of the saloon from behind the abandoned stores across the street. It was in the doorway of one of these stores that they had seen the silhouettes of two men.

"Gone," Bat said, when they had checked all the doorways.

"I have an idea," Clint said, "but we'll have to split up."

"Go ahead."

He told Bat how the two strangers were staying in a boardinghouse at the north end of town, but how one of them frequented a whorehouse at the south end, both owned by a husband and wife.

"And you think these are the two men watching us?"

"I think we should go and ask them."

"I'm game," Bat said. "What do you want, boardinghouse or whorehouse?"

"I'll take the whorehouse," Clint said.

"Why doesn't that surprise me?" Bat asked.

TWENTY-EIGHT

Clint walked to the south end of town and found the whorehouse. It was easy to find, since there were still some lights on inside. Most of the other buildings surrounding it were dark, either because the people were asleep, or because the buildings were abandoned. Clint shook his head when he thought of the number of abandoned buildings he had seen in San Sebastian. If Kenny Witmer was right about this town coming back to life, Clint would have to admit that the man was almost a genius.

He thought about going around to the back of the whorehouse but decided to try the front door first. When he discovered that it was locked, he decided against knocking and announcing himself. He used an alley to work his way around to the back, but in the alley he tripped over something and went sprawling. He lay there for a moment, keeping still and waiting to see if anyone had heard him. When he was sure no one had, he got back to his feet and turned to see what had tripped him up. He was surprised to find that it was a body.

The alley was too dark for him to see who it was, so he dragged the body to the back of the alley with him, where he could use the moonlight to take a better look. As soon as the moonlight struck the body it glinted off the badge on the dead man's chest.

It was Sheriff Montoya.

As near as Clint could tell, the man had been stabbed to death. Clint checked his holster and was surprised to find the man's gun still there.

There was now not even the hint of coincidence, as far as he was concerned. He knew that the sheriff had gone looking for the two strangers, and this meant that he had found them. Hopefully, at least one of them was still inside the whorehouse.

Clint left the body where it was and made his way to the back of the whorehouse.

As Bat Masterson approached the boardinghouse he was not surprised that it was in total darkness. Clint had already told him that the landlord said he had only two guests. One was the man Bat was looking for.

He mounted the steps to the front door and, as expected, found it locked. He quit the porch and worked his way around to the back of the house. The door was locked, but it was flimsy, like most of the buildings in San Sebastian. He took hold of the doorknob, pressed his hip to the door, and pushed until the lock slipped and the door opened.

At the south end of town Clint Adams slipped through the back door of the whorehouse at exactly the same time.

TWENTY-NINE

Bat entered the house and saw that he was in the kitchen. He closed the door behind him, but it remained ajar because it was damaged. As he turned around he saw a light in the hallway and heard footsteps. He had no place to hide, so he stood his ground and waited.

A few seconds later a tremendously fat man entered the kitchen. He stopped short when he saw Bat.

"There's no money here," the man said. "The money is at my wife's whorehouse, at the other end of town."

"I don't want your money."

"I thought you was kind of well dressed to be a thief," the man said. "If you don't want money, then what do you want?"

"You have two guests staying here."

"One," the man said. "The other one stays at the whorehouse. Are you here to kill them?"

"No," Bat said, "just to talk."

"Well," the fat man said, "I'm going to have a snack before I go to sleep. The man you're looking for is upstairs, first door on the right."

"Is he there now?"

"He should be. He just came in a little while ago. Go on up."

"You're going to stay down here?"

"Don't worry," the fat man said, "I'm not gonna get in your way. Only . . . should I send for the sheriff if I hear a shot?"

"No," Bat said, "there won't be any need for the sheriff—especially not if you hear a shot."

"Good," the man said, "I wouldn't want to have to interrupt my snack."

"You don't seem upset about possibly losing a guest," Bat said.

"What the hell's the difference?" the fat man asked. "My wife's whorehouse brings in most of the money. Anyway, he paid in advance. I'm gonna eat now. I'm told it's not a pretty sight, so you probably wouldn't want to watch."

"Enjoy it," Bat said, and left the kitchen. That sounded like a warning he should heed.

He went down the hall the man had come from until he reached a stairway. At the top there was the faint glow of light, as if the man had lit a lamp. Bat took his gun from his holster and started up the stairs.

Clint entered the whorehouse through the back door. When his eyes adjusted to the darkness he saw he was in a long hallway. The place smelled of a mixture of girl's perfumes and just a hint of something stronger . . . and sour. He moved down the hall until he came to the front foyer. The sitting room adjacent to it was filled with plush sofas which, a few hours earlier, had probably had lovely young women in various stages of dress and undress sitting on them.

He looked up the stairs and saw that there were still a few lights on. He could go up and if he was caught pretend to be a customer. How was he going to find the stranger he was looking for, though? He didn't even know what the strangers looked like, after having only gotten a glance at them earlier in the week.

He decided there was nothing to do but go on up and see what happened.

Bat went up the steps quietly, and when he reached the top he saw the light under the first door on the right. Before approaching the door, however, he checked out the rest of the floor. He wanted to make sure there were no surprises waiting for him. Once he was satisfied that the rest of the floor was empty he went back to the door with the light. He briefly considered knocking, then shrugged, backed up, and kicked out. His heel caught the door just below the doorknob and in that split second he realized that the door had probably been unlocked.

The door slammed open and he stepped in with his gun held at the ready. A man was sitting on the bed with his boots off and his gun hanging on the bedpost. Bat was surprised that he never made a move for it.

"*Qué pasa?*" he asked.

"Just sit still, friend."

"Who are you?" Mendez asked.

"My name is Bat Masterson."

"Ah," the man said, "I have heard of you. What can I do for you?"

"I want to talk to you about Eddie Pillman, and a poker game."

''Pillman?'' the man said, frowning. ''Is this a man I am supposed to know?''

''I hope you know him,'' Bat said. ''I think you killed him. It'd be a shame if you killed a man you didn't even know.''

''I have killed many men, señor,'' Mendez said. ''Some I knew, some I did not. In the end I have found it doesn't really matter.''

''Well, this one matters to me.''

''Was he a friend of yours, this Pillman?''

''No.''

''Then why do you care?''

''A friend of mine cares,'' Bat said. ''His name is Clint Adams.''

''Ah,'' Mendez said, ''this name I do know. Why does he care?''

''I think I'll ask the rest of the questions, *compadre*,'' Bat said. ''Like do you know a man named Ken Witmer? And what do you know about a poker game that's taking place here in town?''

But the man didn't seem concerned with these questions, and Bat thought he knew why. He'd seen that look in men's eyes before.

Mendez just stared back and then said, ''The great Bat Masterson.''

He was thinking that if he killed Bat Masterson he would be very famous.

Bat could tell that this was what the man was thinking.

''Don't do it.''

The man stared.

''Don't even think about it, friend,'' Bat said. ''It's not worth dying over.''

''Señor . . .'' Mendez said, and threw himself off the bed.

The move surprised Bat. He had to admit later that Mendez had made a good try of it. Instead of going for his gun right away, as Bat expected he would, he threw himself off the bed, then reached up for the gun. Bat's first shot shattered Mendez's wrist, but the man wouldn't quit, again surprising Bat with his persistence. He reached for the gun with his other hand, drew it from the holster before Bat decided that he had to kill him. He fired again, drilling him through the forehead. The bullet came out the back of his head, spattering the wall with blood and brain matter.

Bat walked over to the body and stared down at it, shaking his head. Did this necessarily make the man guilty of Pillman's killing? No, and now they wouldn't be able to question him.

He hoped Clint would have better luck with his man.

THIRTY

Tino Rosario looked down at Aurora, his favorite whore. In point of fact, the entire whorehouse had only two whores. This one was his favorite because she was meaty, and the other was thin. Also, the other was blond, and Rosario did not like blond women.

He looked down at Aurora, at her fleshy breasts, her brown nipples, her cushiony belly, her heavy thighs. He longed to turn her over and drive his manhood between the cheeks of her solid ass where she was wonderfully tight, but the way he had her tied to the bed made that impossible.

"Please, señor," she said, "untie me, I will give you much pleasure."

It was unfortunate that the whore had seen him use his knife on the lawman. The sheriff had come closer and closer to the bed, all the while staring pop-eyed at Aurora's breasts, until Rosario was finally able to lunge forward and gut him right through the sheet. When the sheriff fell to his knees, Rosario had then slit his throat, finishing the job.

After that he sprang off the bed and grabbed Aurora before she could scream. He thought about killing her right there and then, but he still had use for her. He decided to tie her to the bed and gag her. That done he had dropped the sheriff's body out the window, into the alley below, where he felt it would not be found until daylight. By then he and Mendez would have thought of something to do with it.

That done he had left the whorehouse by the same window and met up with Mendez across the street from the saloon. When the players all left the saloon, he and Mendez had split up again, and he had come back here.

Now he was circling the bed, wondering what he should do to her before he killed her. Once he did kill her he knew he'd have to kill the other whore, too, and the fat bitch who owned the whorehouse. Luckily there were no other customers in the place. In fact, Rosario suspected that right now the fat bitch and the skinny blonde were probably in bed together. After all, what man in his right mind would have the fat one?

"Please, señor," the whore said, "I will say nothing about the sheriff."

He had taken off her gag, just in case he wanted to use her mouth. She had not screamed because he'd threatened to kill her if she did.

"I will slit open your belly so that no one can save you," he had said, "and you will die slowly."

That had scared her and she never screamed. She did, however, continue to plead with him, and he was becoming tired of her pleas.

He decided to use her mouth, just to quiet her down.

• • •

When Clint reached the upper floor he heard the sounds one would expect to hear in a whorehouse. A woman gasping, a man grunting, and bedsprings creaking. He found it odd, however, that all of these sounds were coming from one room. In a town where the boardinghouse had only one guest, was it possible that the whorehouse had only one customer? Maybe even one whore?

He started for the door he thought the sounds were coming from, but in passing another door he heard something else. He stopped and pressed his ear to the door. He heard heavy breathing and much movement, but he did not hear the sound of a man's grunts. He grasped the doorknob and turned it slowly, then eased the door open. He looked inside. A lamp was turned very low, but in the glow of it he could see two naked figures on the bed. He could not make out their faces, but he did see two sets of breasts—one set very small, one set huge and floppy—and two naked butts—one very skinny, and one very wide. It soon became apparent to him that there were two women on the bed together, and they were much too busy with each other to notice him. He knew that the fat woman must have been the boardinghouse man's wife. He wondered if the husband knew what she did with her girls—or if he even cared.

He closed the door quietly and quickly went to the others on the floor, pressing his ear to them. He heard nothing to indicate that anyone was inside. He turned and went back to the first door.

He listened at this one and distinctly heard a man and a woman grunting and moaning. Once again he tried the doorknob and turned it easily. He drew his gun and peered into the room. He could see a naked man from the back, his ass pumping back and forth. He saw the woman beneath him, saw her legs spread wide, her ankles tied to the base of the bed. He could see the hairy thatch between her legs, and knew that the man was fucking her someplace else.

"Just slow down, friend, and take it easy."

"Wha—" the man said.

Clint moved to one side so he could see the man. He saw that he was right, the man's penis was in the woman's mouth, and her face was red, as if she was having a hard time breathing.

On the bedpost hung the man's holster, and there was a knife in a sheath on the belt, as well. Probably the knife that was used to kill the sheriff.

"Señor," the man said, "as you can see I am very busy."

"I can see that." He could also see that the woman's wrists were also tied to the bedposts.

"If you have business with me, perhaps we can conduct it at another time, eh? This *chica* is impatient for me."

"Why don't you take your dick out of her mouth and let the *chica* speak for herself, huh?"

"You don't want to hear what she has to say, señor. She is very *estúpido*."

Clint saw that there were some bloodstains on the sheet beneath them.

"Or maybe you don't want me to hear what she says because she saw you kill the sheriff, huh?"

"Wha—oh, the blood?" the man asked. "Is nothing. She was a virgin before I—"

"Just take your dick out of her mouth, friend."

"Señor—aaiiie!"

It took Clint a moment to realize what had happened. The woman had become impatient, or perhaps she took offense at being called stupid, and had done the only thing she could.

She bit him.

Hard!

The man tried to pull his dick from her mouth, but she was holding on tight. Clint saw blood begin to seep from her mouth, and his ass clenched as he imagined the pain the man was feeling.

"Get her off, get her off!" the man screamed.

Clint was about to say something when the man reached for his gun, obviously intending to shoot the woman.

"Hey, wait—" Clint shouted, but the man was beyond hearing. He drew his gun from the holster and started to bring it to bear on the woman. Clint had no choice.

He shot him.

The man screamed—whether from the bullet or the pain in his crotch, Clint didn't know—and died. He approached the bed as the man went limp, and looked underneath him at the woman.

"You can let go now, ma'am," he said. "He's dead."

The woman spit the man's almost severed penis from her mouth, took a deep breath, and screamed.

Clint didn't blame her.

THIRTY-ONE

Clint left the whorehouse, telling the three women to leave the body of the man in the room and close the door, someone would be along to collect him in the morning.

He went into the alley and slung the body of the sheriff over his shoulder. Not knowing where to take him, he carried him back to the hotel and deposited him in one of the chairs out front. At that point Bat came along and watched, his arms folded, as Clint propped the man up.

"What happened?" Bat asked.

"My guy killed the sheriff."

"And?"

"I had to kill him."

"That's great."

"Why?"

"My guy went for his gun, and I had to kill him."

Clint straightened up.

"So we don't know if they killed Pillman."

"No."

"But we do know—from one of the whores at the whorehouse—that my guy killed the sheriff. She saw him."

"And he let her live?"

"He tied her to the bed. I guess he was going to use her some more before he killed her."

"Not very smart."

"I guess neither one of them was," Clint said, "but I think they killed Pillman."

"Well," Bat said, "we can decide to believe that, I guess."

Ken Witmer came out of the hotel and stopped short at the sight of the dead man.

"What happened?"

They explained it to him.

"So they killed Pillman?"

"We think so," Clint said.

"So we can go on with the game tomorrow and not worry about anything."

"You can worry about where you're going to get your next sheriff from," Clint said.

"Well, how about—"

"No," Clint said.

"Bat, what about—"

"Don't even think about it!"

"Fine," Witmer said, "I won't even think about it until after the game. Maybe this town has a council, or something."

"Good luck," Bat said.

"Kenny, I want you to take a look at the two dead men in the morning."

"What for?"

"To see if you know them."

"Why would I?"

"Just do it," Clint said.

"Okay, fine," Witmer said, "I'll start my day off by looking at two dead men. Can we get some sleep now?"

"Sure," Clint said, "why not."

"Are you gonna leave him there like that?" Witmer asked, pointing to the dead sheriff.

"In the morning we can get some men to move all three bodies," Clint said. "For now we'll just have to leave them all where they are."

The three men entered the hotel, and Bat started telling Clint about how his man had actually surprised him. . . .

THIRTY-TWO

In the morning, after breakfast, Clint and Ken Witmer went to find out if San Sebastian had a town council. As it turned out they did, and they also had a mayor, who also owned the general store.

The mayor's name was Walter Meyers, and he was shocked to hear of the death of the sheriff.

"Goddamn it," he said from behind a huge mustache with waxed ends. He had dark hair that was rapidly receding, and looked to be about forty. "Who's gonna be sheriff now?"

"Hire somebody," Clint said.

"Who would want to be sheriff of this one-horse town?" the mayor asked.

"Mayor, if you'll allow me, I'd like to help," Witmer said. "I own the saloon now—"

"I know that, Mr. Witmer," Meyers said. "We were going to ask you if you would sit on the town council."

"I'd be honored," Witmer said. "How many members are there?"

"There's me, the sheriff, and now you," Meyers said. Then he slapped his forehead with his palm and said, "Oh, hell, I guess there's just you and me now that the sheriff's gone."

"No one else?" Witmer asked.

"No one."

"Well," Witmer said, "there will be, once this town gets on its feet again."

Mayor Meyers laughed.

"What's so funny?" Clint asked.

"W-what your friend said about getting this town on its feet again."

"Why is that funny?" Clint asked.

"Mister," Meyers said, "San Sebastian ain't never *been* on its feet before."

They left the mayor with the task of getting some men to remove all of the dead bodies and take them to the undertaker.

"At least we got an undertaker," he said.

"And he's been busy lately," Clint said, as they left the general store.

Outside Clint said to Witmer, "It looks like you might actually have a say in who becomes sheriff of this town. That is, if you're still going to stay here."

"I'm staying, Clint," Witmer said. "Mark my words, this town is going to grow."

"I hope you're right," Clint said. "Come on, let's go take a look at the other two dead men."

"Ah, I just had breakfast—"

"Kenny!"

"Okay, okay," Witmer said, "I'll look."

• • •

First they went to the whorehouse to give Witmer a look at the man Clint had killed and then to the boardinghouse for a look at the other one.

That done they started back to the hotel.

"Know them?"

"No," Witmer said.

"You're a damned liar, Kenny."

"Wha—"

"I saw your face when you looked at those two men," Clint said. "You recognized both of them."

"Well . . . I might have—"

"Might have from where?"

Witmer looked unhappy.

"I think they work for Don Carlos."

"You mean . . . your future father-in-law?"

Witmer nodded.

"What would they be doing here?"

"Well . . ."

"Come on, Kenny!"

"There's something I didn't tell you, Clint."

"What a surprise. Like what?"

"Well . . . Don Carlos isn't exactly happy about me marrying his daughter."

"Describe 'not exactly happy' for me, Kenny."

Witmer looked down.

"He said he'd kill me before he'd let me marry her."

"Oh, that's great," Clint said. "So he probably sent these men here to kill you."

"Maybe."

"And maybe they got interested in the money from the game."

"Maybe."

"What's he going to do when he finds out they failed?" Clint asked.

"I don't—"

"I do," Clint said. "He'll send some more men. Kenny, why do you want to marry this woman if her father will kill you for it?"

"I love her, Clint."

Clint stopped.

"Look at me and say that."

Witmer stopped, turned to Clint, looked him in the eye and said, "I love her."

Clint stared at him for a few moments.

"You're not lying, are you, you little shit?"

"No, I'm not."

Clint hesitated a moment, then said, "Hell, let's go get this game finished."

THIRTY-THREE

When the players were all assembled, Witmer made an announcement that Pillman's killers had not only been caught, but killed by Clint and Bat Masterson. He left out the part about the sheriff being killed, and he left out the fact that nobody was dead *sure* that these men had killed Eddie Pillman.

"Well," Hiram Excess said, "now that that's settled, can we play cards?"

"By all means," Witmer said.

They sat down and Jo Dillon was the first dealer. They let Waco go, paying him off because they didn't need three dealers. Kendall Will and Jo would now alternate.

"I guess you don't need me anymore, Clint," Bear Wilcox said.

"No, Bear," Clint said, "you can stay or go, whatever you want to do."

"To tell you the truth," Wilcox said, "I don't particularly want to see who ends up with my money, so I think I'll be going."

"Fine."

Wilcox left and Clint locked the door behind him. He went back to the bar, got a beer from Culley, and started nursing it while he watched the game.

The next player to drop out of the game was Hiram Excess.

"I was in that game longer than I thought anyway," he said as Clint let him out. "I had some streak of luck there for a while, but it didn't last."

"It never does, Hiram."

That left Bat Masterson, Gentleman Jim Everett, Doc Kennedy, and Ken Witmer in the game. From Clint's vantage point he could see that most of the chips were in front of Witmer and Bat. Doc Kennedy seemed to be doing okay, but Gentleman Jim's stake was dwindling.

"How about dealer's choice?" Gentleman Jim asked at one point. "I'm kind of sick of five-card stud, and with only four players . . ."

"Anyone object?" Witmer asked.

No one did. In fact, they each appreciated the opportunity to introduce their favorite, or best, game into the mix.

While Jo Dillon did the physical dealing, they kept track of whose deal it would have been, and that person called the game. Pretty soon it broke down this way: When it was Bat's game he played seven-card stud, Gentleman Jim preferred draw poker, Doc Kennedy kept playing five-card stud, and Witmer mixed his games.

Changing the games didn't help Gentleman Jim. By five-thirty that evening he was out of the game, after a particularly brutal hand.

Clint watched as Jo dealt each player five cards around the table. Bat, then Doc, then Witmer, and finally Gentleman Jim. The game was anything to open, but Bat passed anyway, which told Clint he had a particularly bad hand.

"Open for fifty," Doc said.

"Call," Witmer said.

"Raise a hundred," Gentleman Jim said. He either had a good hand or he was trying to force something. He didn't have all that many chips in front of him.

"I'm out," Bat said, and sat back to watch, leaving his cards facedown on the table.

"Call the raise," Doc said.

"Call," Witmer said.

"Cards?" Jo asked.

"Two," Doc said.

Knowing Doc as he did, Clint felt sure that Doc had opened with three of a kind.

"Three," Witmer said.

"I'll play these," Gentleman Jim said.

Was he bluffing or had he been dealt a pat hand?

"The bet is to Doc," Jo said.

Doc apparently didn't care that Jim had a pat hand, for he said, "Bet a hundred."

Witmer looked at Jim, as if trying to figure out what he had. Clint thought he should probably worry more about Doc.

"I'll raise fifty," he finally said. Calling the bet probably would have been a waste of time, because with a pat hand Gentleman Jim had to raise. Maybe by raising himself, though, Witmer was trying to throw Jim off.

"I call, and raise two hundred," Gentleman Jim said.

"Call both raises," Doc said, "and raise five hundred."

Witmer pressed his lips together. He wanted to stay in the game, but five hundred worth?

"Fold," he said reluctantly.

"Call the five hundred," Jim said, "and . . . I've got a hundred and ninety left. That's the raise."

"Hundred and ninety to you, Doc," Jo said.

"I'll call the raise," Doc said.

"Jim?" Jo asked.

"Flush, king high," Jim said, spreading his cards.

"Doc?"

Doc Kennedy spread his cards on the table, revealing three jacks over two eights.

"Full house."

"Beats the pat hand," Jo said.

Doc looked at Jim and spread his hands in a helpless gesture.

"Gentleman Jim is out of the game," Jo announced.

Jim stood up, took Jo's hand, and kissed it. Then he executed a slight bow and said, "Gentlemen, thank you for an interesting game."

At that point they broke, and Culley put out sandwiches to go with beer and coffee. Gentleman Jim stayed to eat, and wanted to see the outcome of the game.

Gentleman Jim walked over to where Clint was standing, shaking his head.

"Tough game," Clint said.

"What else could I do?" Jim asked. "I was dealt a flush, for Chrissake."

"Have a drink, Jim," Clint said. "On the house."

"Least you could do," Jim said, and moved away, still shaking his head.

"Down to three players," Witmer said, coming up alongside Clint.

"You're doing pretty well, Ken. Looks like you've got most of the chips."

"Bat's a little ahead of me," Witmer said, "but I'm holding my own."

''How long do you think Doc will last?'' Clint asked.

''Not much longer,'' Witmer said. ''His luck has gone sour.''

''He just took that hand with some luck.''

Witmer shook his head.

''That was Jim's bad luck, not Doc's good luck. Doc's about done.''

''So it will come down to you and Bat, huh?''

''Looks like it.''

''Are you ready for that?''

''Oh yeah,'' Witmer said, rubbing his hands together. ''I'm ready. In spite of everything that's been going on, I've been getting my confidence back with each hand. I think I'm ready to go head-to-head with Bat Masterson.''

Clint thought that when the game came down to two people the stakes would go up, otherwise it could take forever. He'd seen Bat play head-to-head before, and he had a lot of patience. He wondered how Witmer would respond to the pressure.

When Witmer went to get a sandwich Bat came over, holding a beer.

''Your friend looks excited.''

''He is.''

''He should be,'' Bat said. ''He's getting some good cards. Kennedy'll be out soon and then it'll be Witmer and me.''

''He feels good, Bat,'' Clint said. ''He feels like he's ready to go against you.''

''If the cards go against me,'' Bat said, ''he has a chance. If we both keep getting good cards, I'll outlast him.''

Clint knew that Bat didn't often leave things to luck. He'd press the game by betting high, or bluffing, or just generally trying to affect Witmer's thinking by doing the unexpected.

When they sat back down to play, it was Kendall Will's deal. Jo stayed in the room to watch, standing next to Clint and nursing one of her drinks. Gentleman Jim stood at one end of the bar with a beer, watching intently.

They played for two more hours, with Bat and Witmer taking most of the hands. Doc Kennedy won a hand every now and then to keep him in the game, but eventually his luck ran out.

"Gentlemen," Doc said, standing up, "I thank you for a most interesting time, and wish you the best of luck."

"Thanks, Doc," Witmer said. Bat simply nodded. He and Witmer played on. . . .

They played for four more hours and virtually alternated hands. The size of their stacks of chips did not significantly increase or diminish. Then there was a turning point, a decisive hand that Bat took because Witmer thought he was bluffing.

Clint knew that Witmer had a strong hand by the way he was playing, and sitting. He knew Bat saw it, too. Neither of them had noticed it before because there had been so many players in the game, but apparently Witmer had been away from the game for so long that he had developed a tell—and a rather obvious one, at that. He sat up much straighter when he had a good hand.

Witmer felt this hand was so good that he increased his betting, and in the end he fell short when his jacks full over threes was beaten by Bat's kings full over tens.

"Bat's got him now," Jo said.

That remained to be seen, Clint thought.

THIRTY-FOUR

Little by little the advantage seemed to have shifted to Bat, although it was not obvious by any means that Bat *had* Witmer.

They took another break at midnight so the players and dealers could stretch their legs, and backs, and fingers, and whatever else had stiffened or cramped up.

Standing off to one side with Clint, Bat said, ''He's developed a tell.''

''I noticed.''

''Still,'' Bat said, ''it's taking me longer than I thought. I might have to open up my game a bit.''

''That should be interesting.''

''It's already too interesting,'' Bat said sourly. ''I should have had him beat by now.''

''Could it be he's a better player than you thought?'' Clint asked teasingly.

''He *might* have been a better player than I thought before he developed this tell,'' Bat said. ''In the end, that's what's going to beat him.''

Bat and Witmer went back to the table, and Jo was dealing. Even Kendall Will, who showed little interest in the game when he wasn't dealing, stayed around to watch the developments.

Bat seemed to be assuming the upper hand, although not as obviously as Jo Dillon seemed to be thinking earlier. Then, just like that, the cards turned and Witmer started to beat Bat—though just barely.

After a hard fought hand Bat lost with kings when Witmer had aces.

In another hand Bat filled an inside straight, only to lose to a flush.

And in still another, with both men betting heavily, Bat had fours and Witmer had fives.

It was at this point in a game when Clint would get up and walk away from the table. When the cards started coming like this, there was nothing you could do *but* quit.

Except in a game like this, where there was no quitting.

Things evened out after that, but there were more chips on Witmer's side of the table now than on Bat's.

At one point, when Jo was shuffling, Clint walked over to the table and asked, ''Do you fellas want to take a break? It's almost daylight.''

''I'm for going on,'' Bat said. ''Might as well get it over with.''

''I agree,'' Witmer said.

''Have it your way,'' Clint said. ''Deal, Jo.''

Jo dealt out a hand of five-card stud, and immediately everyone in the room felt that something was going to happen. Bat got two kings, while Witmer was dealt a ten and jack of clubs. Bat's kings were a heart and a club.

''A hundred,'' Bat said.

"Call."

The next card came out, and it was another king for Bat. Witmer drew a queen of clubs. Three cards to a straight flush against three kings. There was no way Witmer could make a royal flush, though, because Bat had his king.

"Let's see if we can't get this over with," Bat said. "Five thousand."

"Raise two," Witmer said immediately.

Both Clint and Bat looked at Witmer slouching in his chair and felt that he was bluffing. It was a good move on Witmer's part, to look as if he didn't care that Bat had suddenly sent the game into another phase.

"Call your two and raise four," Bat said.

Three kings or four, Clint thought, they were still worth the raise.

"Call your four," Witmer said.

He's waiting for his last card, Clint thought. If he makes his straight flush his back will straighten also.

Bat's last card was a three. If he had a king in the hole, he had his four kings.

Witmer's card was an eight of clubs. He had an eight, ten, jack, and queen of clubs showing. He needed to have the nine in the hole for the straight flush. Clint watched him as he peered at his hole card again and he remained slouched in his seat.

"Your bet, Bat," Jo said.

"Ten thousand," Bat said.

"Raise ten," Witmer said without hesitation.

"You're bluffing, Witmer," Bat said.

"Prove it, Bat."

Twenty-four players had started the game, with a five-thousand-dollar each buy-in. That made the entire pot 120,000.

Bat looked at the chips he had in front of him.

"I've got about nine thousand left in front of me, Witmer," Bat said. "That's the bet."

He pushed it into the pot. Jo counted it and announced, "Ninety-four hundred."

Witmer had more than that in front of him, but he said, "I'll call the bet, Bat. Your ninety-four hundred."

Bat turned over the king of diamonds.

"Bat has four kings," Jo said.

Witmer hesitated just a moment, then turned over the nine of clubs. Clint heard Gentleman Jim and Doc Kennedy both suck in their breaths.

"Straight flush," Jo said hoarsely.

Bat glared at Witmer and said, "You used a false tell, didn't you?"

"I used a straight flush, Bat," Witmer said. "That was what I needed to beat you, and that's what I got."

Clint watched Bat carefully. Of course Witmer had created a false tell, and both he and Bat had fallen for it. He wanted to be ready for any reaction on Bat's part.

Bat stood up, finally, then reached his hand across the table to Witmer.

"Well played."

Witmer seemed touched by the gesture. He stood and shook Bat's hand.

"Thanks, Bat."

"I need some sleep," Bat said, "and then some food, and then I'm out of this town."

Clint came over and said, "It was a good game, Bat."

"Yeah," Bat said, "it was. Your friend, there, hornswoggled me."

"Me, too, Bat," Clint said. "Me, too."

"See you before I leave," Bat said.

Clint unlocked the front door so Bat, Gentleman Jim, Doc Kennedy, Jo Dillon, and Kendall Will could leave.

Then he walked to the table, where Witmer was gathering his chips.

"You did it," he said.

"I did, didn't I?"

"That false tell was a great idea, Ken."

"What tell?"

"Come on," Clint said. "All day you've been sitting straight as an arrow whenever you got a good hand."

"I was?"

"You know you were."

"All I know is I won," Witmer said. "That's all that counts."

"You're not going to admit it, are you?"

"Admit what?" Witmer asked.

"Okay, forget it," Clint said. "You've got your money. Now you can fix this place up, but what good is that going to do if the town doesn't come to life?"

"It will," Witmer said. "Maybe I've got the money, but the last part of my plan is for the town to grow—and it will."

"With all this money you won I guess you don't need me anymore."

Witmer put his hand out and grabbed the front of Clint's shirt, as if to keep him from running off.

"No, no, I still need you, Clint," he said. "We had a deal. You're my partner."

"If you want me for a partner you'll have to tell me how much money you want from me to buy in with."

"I don't need any money from you," Witmer said, "not now. I've got the money I need. I just need you as my partner, Clint, that's all. I need that in order to keep myself in line."

Clint took a deep breath and said, "All right, Kenny. I'm your partner for a year."

"A year," Witmer said, "unless you want to stay on after that. Is it a deal now?" He stuck out his hand.

"Okay," Clint said, taking it, "it's a deal."

THIRTY-FIVE

One month later . . .

When Clint rode into San Sebastian he couldn't believe his eyes. There were people walking the streets, and many of the buildings had undergone repairs. In some cases whole new buildings existed where before there were abandoned, falling down ones.

When he came within sight of the saloon he reined Duke in and stared. The sign above the door read, THE PALACE, and the front of the building had undergone a complete makeover.

It had been a month since he left town after the poker game. He had gone back to Labyrinth, then into New Mexico to help a friend who was in trouble. When he returned to Labyrinth there was a message from Ken Witmer asking him to come back to San Sebastian.

"You won't believe your eyes," Ken had said in the telegram, and he was right.

Before Clint left Labyrinth, his friend Rick Hartman had shown him an article in a copy of an Austin, Texas, newspaper. The headline read, TOWN COMES TO LIFE, and it was the story of the rebirth of a town called San Sebastian. A couple of big ranches had appeared nearby, and they were doing business with other big ranches across the border in Mexico. The articles also credited the appearance of a gambling hall called the Palace with drawing people into San Sebastian. It even mentioned the name of the owner of the Palace, Kenneth Witmer. It didn't once mention that Clint was a partner, which suited him just fine.

Now that he saw what he was a partner in he wondered if this wasn't something he'd want to hang on to when his promised year was up.

Clint left Duke at the livery and went directly to the saloon. Since he was a partner he didn't need to take a hotel room. There'd be a room above the saloon for him.

When he walked in he stopped and stared. There were crystal chandeliers where previously there had been bare ceilings. The old, chipped bar had been replaced by one of polished mahogany. Even the spittoons on the floor glowed and shone.

There were gaming tables all around. He saw roulette, faro, poker, blackjack, red dog, even a wheel of fortune, and at each table there was little more than elbow room.

Walking around the room, serving drinks and talking with the customers, were three very pretty girls, one brunette, one blonde, and one redhead. They all looked to be in their twenties, and all had bosoms that were overflowing from their low-cut dresses.

As Clint approached the bar, Culley saw him and came to greet him with a handshake.

"How ya doin', boss?"

"Hello, Culley."

"This is somethin', huh?" Culley said proudly, putting his hands on his hips.

"I'll say it's something."

"The boss knows what he's doin' after all, don't he?" Culley asked.

"It sure looks like it. Where is Kenny, Culley?"

"He's in the office. Want me to have your rifle and saddlebags taken up to your room?"

"Huh? Oh, sure, thanks."

Clint put the rifle and saddlebags on the bar and walked to the office door. He knocked before entering. Witmer was sitting behind his desk, going over some books. Near to his hand was a lit cigar sitting in an ashtray. The last time Clint had seen this room it had been mostly empty, very dusty, and filled with guns taken from the poker players.

Witmer looked up when the door opened and smiled widely when he saw Clint.

"There's my partner!" he said, bounding to his feet.

He charged across the room and grabbed Clint's hand.

"I'm really glad to see you, Clint. What do you think of the place?"

"Kenny . . . I don't know what to say," Clint replied. "The place . . . the whole town . . . how did you know?"

Witmer touched his nose and said, "I didn't know, Clint, but I smelled money. My nose is always right."

"This place is amazing," Clint said.

"And it's a gold mine. I've opened an account for you at the bank, and your profits have been going in there. Want to see the books?"

"I don't need to see any books, Kenny," Clint said. "I trust you. And what profits are you talking about? I didn't even make an initial investment."

"You've invested your time," Witmer said, "and your confidence, Clint. That's good enough for me. Come on, sit down. Let me tell you what's been going on."

He showed Clint to a chair and then handed him a glass of brandy.

"I've read about some of what's been going on," Clint said.

"That's right," Witmer said, "we've been making the newspapers. Our population has quadrupled, Clint, and we now have a dozen members on the town council. We have a new mayor, too."

"You?"

"No, not me," Witmer said. "They wanted me to run, but I said no. It's somebody you don't know, one of the new residents. We had an election and he won. His name is Cooper, Harvey Cooper. He's a much better mayor than that Meyers was, let me tell you. He's gone, by the way. Pulled out when he lost. Sold his store. Said the town was getting too crowded for him."

Clint sipped his brandy and listened, for want of something better to do at the moment.

"There's another saloon in town, but that's okay. They don't have any gambling, and they're not much competition. We'll have another hotel, too."

"What about the boardinghouse?"

"Oh, that's still here, and so is the whorehouse—although it's got six girls now, and they're all attractive. *Everything* around here is more attractive, isn't it?"

"I guess so . . ."

"What'd you think of the girls out front?" Witmer asked. "Pretty, huh? Got five of them working, and they all look like that."

"Five girls? Can we afford that?"

"We can afford that and more. Business is booming, Clint!"

"What about the other problem?"

"What other problem?"

"You know . . . Don Carlos? Not wanting you to marry Carmen?"

"Oh, that," Witmer said. "I solved that."

"You did?"

"Well, sort of."

"What do you mean, sort of?"

"Well . . . I kinda called off the wedding."

"You didn't marry her?"

"Would I have married her without my partner here?" Witmer asked. "You would have been my best man."

"Okay, then you're not going to marry her?"

"No."

"How did she take the news?"

"She was heartbroken . . . I guess."

"What do you mean, you guess?"

"I sent her a telegram."

"You broke it off with her by telegram?"

"Yeah. I was too busy to leave town to do it."

"Kenny . . ."

"I know, I know, I shouldn't have done it that way, but I did."

"Well, it must have made her father happy."

"Sort of. . . ."

Clint rolled his eyes.

"What do you mean, sort of?"

"Well, the word I get is he wants to kill me."

"What? But he didn't want you to marry her."

"I know," Witmer said, "but now he seems to think I besmirched her honor by dumping her."

''Has he sent anyone to try to kill you?''

''No,'' Witmer said, ''not since those last two, but I'm expecting it.''

''What are you doing about security?''

''I carry a gun, and Culley still has his shotgun behind the bar.''

''That reminds me,'' Clint said. ''Does this town have a sheriff now?''

''Oh, yes, we replaced Montoya. The sheriff's name is Kennedy—Doc Kennedy.''

''What? Doc took the job?''

''Turns out he likes it here—or he did, when the town was quiet. I think he's getting a bit antsy, too, now that the town is growing.''

''I didn't know Doc had ever worn a badge.''

''He never did,'' Witmer said. ''This is the first time.''

''Is he any good?''

''He hasn't had to do much yet,'' Witmer said. ''It's been a pretty law-abiding town so far.''

''Well, if Don Carlos sends some men to this side of the border after your head he'll have to do something.''

''Oh, he knows that,'' Witmer said. ''I've told him all about that. He checks out all the strangers who come into town. Maybe you should go and see him.''

''What for?''

''To give him some pointers.''

''I don't think Doc would want any pointers from me,'' Clint said, ''but maybe I'll go and see him just to let him know I'm here.''

''That sounds like a good idea. Did Culley take your stuff to your room?''

''He did.''

''Good. You'll like your room a lot.''

''I'm sure I will.''

"You can take a bath in the back. Just tell Culley, and he'll have someone get you some hot water."

"I think I'll do that first," Clint said. "Then I'll take a look around town and go and see Doc."

"Good," Witmer said. "Come back here later and we'll have some dinner together. I've still got a lot more to tell you."

Clint stood up, leaving his brandy on the desk.

"I think I've got a lot to take in already."

"Hey," Witmer said, spreading his arms, "it just keeps getting better."

"I'll see you later, Kenny."

Clint went outside, asked Culley to arrange for the bath, then went up to his room for some clean clothes. Maybe a nice hot bath would stop his head from spinning.

THIRTY-SIX

Clint followed Culley's directions and found the room that had been set up as a bathhouse in the back of the building. He remembered that a month ago it had been a storage room.

There was one bathtub and it was already filled with hot water. On a chair near the tub was a clean towel. Clint stripped off his dirty clothes and eased himself into the hot water. He leaned back and rested his head against the back of the porcelain tub. Closing his eyes, he let the water seep into his muscles. He wanted to soak a bit before he soaped himself. He was drifting off when he heard the door open.

"Who is it?" he asked.

His gun was on the chair next to the towel and he reached for it.

"You won't need your gun," a woman's voice said.

"Wha—"

She came into view and he recognized her. She was the

blonde who had been working the saloon when he walked in. Up close he could see that she was extremely pretty and well built, particularly her arms and her chest. Her blond hair was long, but she had it pinned up.

"My name's Holly."

"Hi, Holly."

"I understand you're my other boss."

"I guess I am."

"Well, Mr. Witmer asked me to come back here and help you."

"Help me with what?"

She shrugged, smiled, and said, "I guess he wants me to wash your back, or something."

"Holly," Clint said, "I really appreciate the offer, but I can wash my own back."

"What?"

"I mean you don't have to do anything you don't want to do," Clint said. "Your job doesn't depend on you washing my back."

"It doesn't?"

"No, it doesn't. Did Mr. Witmer say it did?"

"Uh, no, but I thought—"

"Do you wash his back when he takes a bath?"

"No," she said, then added, "well, I haven't up to now."

"And the other girls?"

"I don't know."

"Well, you make sure they know what I just told you. Nobody's job depends on satisfying the boss. Okay?"

"Sure," she said. "Uh, are you sure you don't want me to—"

"Holly," Clint said, "you're a very beautiful girl and I would love you to wash my back, but right now I just want to soak. Maybe next time, if you're interested. Okay?"

She stared at him for a few moments, then said, "Can I ask you something?"

"Sure."

"Are you really the Gunsmith?"

"I'm really Clint Adams," he said. "Why?"

"You just don't seem . . . you're not anything like I thought you'd be."

"Is that good, or bad?"

"It's good, I guess," she said. "No, it's very good. I thought you'd be—well, you know, like other men."

"And I'm not?"

"I don't know any other man who would refuse to have me wash his back."

"Well," he said, "you make the offer another time, when I haven't just ridden ten hours, and maybe I'll be like any other man after all."

"I doubt that, Mr. Adams," she said. "I really do."

"Thanks, Holly. I'll see you later, huh?"

"Sure, Mr. Adams."

"And you can call me Clint."

"See you later, Clint."

The beautiful girl left the room, and Clint leaned back. He couldn't believe he'd just sent her away. Maybe he was just getting old.

THIRTY-SEVEN

After his bath Clint went over to see Doc Kennedy.

"Clint," Doc said, coming around his desk. "What brings you here?"

The two men shook hands.

"Just came back to see the changes that have taken place, Doc."

"It's somethin', huh?" Doc asked. "Guess you're surprised to see me wearing this badge, huh?"

"Frankly, yes."

"Well, I probably won't be wearing it much longer," Doc said. "I think the job's on the verge of gettin' too big for me. I'm just a gambler after all."

Clint thought about suggesting that the town might need a good vet, but being a vet always seemed to be a sore spot with Doc Kennedy for some reason.

"Thinking on leaving anytime soon?"

"Oh, I'll probably finish out my term," Doc said. "By

that time the lid should be coming off this town and they'll need a real sheriff. How about you?"

"What, for this job? I don't think so. I haven't worn a badge in a long time, and I don't intend to start again."

"What can I do for you today?" Doc asked.

"I just wanted to let you know I was here, Doc," Clint said. "Also, I wanted to ask about this business with Don Carlos Ortiz."

"Do you take that seriously?" Doc asked.

"Remember Eddie Pillman?"

"Sure."

"Well, he was killed by the two men Don Carlos sent here to kill Ken Witmer."

Of course, Clint wasn't dead sure of that, but he was sure enough.

"I didn't know that," Doc said.

"Kenny didn't tell you?"

"No."

Clint frowned. Maybe Witmer wasn't taking the threat seriously enough after all.

"Do you have any deputies?" Clint asked.

"Two."

"Maybe the three of you could just keep an eye on the saloon and Witmer for a while, huh?"

"What are you gonna do?"

"Well," Clint said, "I don't want to lose a partner, so I guess I'll have to go and see Don Carlos Ortiz."

"Good," Doc said. "If you get that settled it'll be one less thing for us to worry about."

"I'll do my best."

"When will you go?"

"Tomorrow, I think," Clint said. "I just got to town today and I want to rest my horse."

"Well, let me know what happens."

"I will."

Clint left the sheriff's office and took a turn around town before returning to the saloon to have dinner with Witmer.

"You're gonna do what?"

"I'm going to go and have a talk with Don Carlos."

"On my behalf."

"Well, of course—and mine, too. After all, I don't want to lose a partner."

They were sitting in one of the new restaurants that had opened up in San Sebastian, and the place was doing a brisk business. If Witmer hadn't already had a table reserved, they'd still be waiting for one.

Now Kenny took his cloth napkin from his lap and wiped some sauce from his mouth.

"You know, I've never known whether to take this threat seriously or not."

"Why? Why the other one and not this one?"

"Well, the other one was because Don Carlos didn't want me to marry Carmen. I think this one is just a show for her benefit."

"Well, I'll find out for sure by talking to him."

"Maybe that's a good idea, Clint," Witmer said. "After all, Don Carlos is doing a lot business on this side of the border now, with both Sam Dolan and Harry Bittle. They're the two men who have started big ranches nearby. Sooner or later I'm gonna come face-to-face with Don Carlos on the street, and I'll want to know whether I should go for my gun or not."

"Don't go for your gun anytime soon, Kenny," Clint said. "You're a gambler, not a gunfighter."

"I know that."

"Speaking of that," Clint said, "how is your gambling?"

"I have a private game going almost every night," Witmer replied. "I'm fleecing the locals, Clint. They don't have a chance."

"Looks to me like your confidence is all the way back," Clint said.

"No," Witmer said, "not all the way back. There's still one thing I have to do."

"What's that?"

"I'll tell you when you get back from Don Carlos's ranch," Witmer said.

"I'll be going first thing in the morning," Clint said. "All I need is directions."

"That's easy . . ." Witmer said, and started giving them.

THIRTY-EIGHT

Ken Witmer's directions to Don Carlos's rancho were very easy to follow. When Clint came within sight of the house he was impressed. It was a beautiful wood and stucco house with arches and blooming foliage, as lovely a house as anyone could hope for. If he was the kind of man who wanted a place to settle down, this would be very close to perfect for him.

He knew that he had been on Don Carlos's land for some time, but up until now he hadn't seen any men. Now, as he approached the house, five or six men came forward to meet him. They were all ranch hands, but they were all wearing guns.

"Stop there, señor, and state your business," one of them said.

"My name is Clint Adams. I have come to speak with Don Carlos."

"And what is it you wish to speak to the *patrón* about?" the man asked.

"Who am I addressing now?" Clint asked.

The man's back stiffened and his chest puffed out. He was about thirty-five, with a bushy black mustache and a build that was heavy in the upper body.

"I am Felipe Rojas, the foreman of this rancho. You must state your business to me, señor, before you can see the *patrón.*"

"That's fair," Clint said. "I want to talk to him about Kenneth Witmer."

Rojas screwed up his face and then spit on the ground. So much for his opinion of Witmer.

"Stay here, señor," Rojas said. "I will see if the *patrón* will speak with you about that *pendejo.*"

Clint wasn't sure what that meant, but he was fairly certain that it wasn't good.

Rojas walked to the house and entered. He reappeared several minutes later.

"My men will care for your animal, señor. If you will follow me, please?"

Clint wondered why Rojas was suddenly respectful and polite. What had he done to deserve such treatment?

He dismounted and handed Duke's reins to one of the caballeros.

"Be careful," he said, "he'll bite your hand off."

"This way, señor," Rojas said.

Clint followed Rojas into the house, through a large lobby, down a hallway and out the back of the house to a fully furnished portico. There he found Don Carlos sitting in a wicker chair. The man had white hair and a white beard, and a ruddy complexion. He appeared to be in his sixties.

"Señor Adams?"

"That's right."

"Welcome to my house, señor," the man said, though he made no move to shake Clint's hand in welcome. "May I offer you a drink? Whiskey? Something cold? I believe my daughter has made some lemonade."

"Lemonade would be fine."

"Felipe, have Carmen bring some lemonade for myself and my guest."

"*Sí, Patrón.*"

"Please, señor, sit down."

There was another wicker chair and Clint sat in it.

"I know of you, señor. Your reputation precedes you."

"Sometimes I wish it didn't, Don Carlos."

The man smiled.

"I understand that. I, too, have a reputation . . . just a little one, you understand, in my own country."

"I think you are modest, Don Carlos," Clint said. "Your name is spoken with respect on my side of the river."

"*Gracias*," the old man said, inclining his head slightly to accept the compliment. "Please . . . ah, here is the lemonade."

Clint turned and saw the girl entering the portico. She was carrying a tray with a pitcher and two glasses on it. She appeared to be in her early twenties, with long, very black hair and dark, smooth skin. Her lips were full, as was her figure. She was stunning.

"Carmen, please pour for our guest. This is Mr. Adams. Mr. Adams, this is my daughter, my treasure, Carmen."

"*Con mucho gusto*," she said, curtsying ever so slightly.

"I am very pleased to meet you, señorita."

She poured her father and Clint a glass of lemonade each, then stepped back as if awaiting instructions.

"Go now, my sweet. Mr. Adams and I have business to discuss."

"Yes, Papa."

She hastened away.

"She is the very image of her mother, my late wife," Don Carlos said.

"Then your wife must have been very beautiful, Don Carlos."

"Indeed, she was," the old man said, "beautiful, and wise. If only she were here these past few years to help me with Carmen. She is a headstrong girl."

"Don Carlos, I fear I must tell you something that may not make me welcome here."

"Tell it, then."

"I am friends and partners with Kenneth Witmer, to whom I understand your daughter was engaged to marry."

"Yes," Don Carlos said, "she was engaged to that . . . man. However, to subject you to my disapproval of him would not be fair, and so you are wrong. You are still welcome here . . . depending, of course, on what your purpose is."

"My purpose is simple," Clint said. "It is to save the life of my friend."

"Why come to me with this?"

"It is my understanding that you wish him harm."

Suddenly, the old man rose and hurried across the portico floor to the door his daughter had gone through. He looked inside, then came back to his chair. He beckoned Clint to lean closer.

"Perhaps, at one time, this was true, señor. In fact, I made a very bad decision in haste, one that might have turned out much worse than it did. Do you know to what I am referring?"

"I think so," Clint said. The death of the two Mexicans a month earlier, no doubt.

"I am pleased that your friend and partner broke his engagement to my daughter. I was not happy with the way he did it, however. It was cowardly, and it broke her heart."

"I'm sorry."

Don Carlos waved away his apology.

"There is no need," he said. "She will get over it. As for wanting harm to befall your partner, if he were to fall and break an arm or a leg I would not weep, but tell him he has nothing to fear from me. I will send no one to do him harm."

"I hope I am correct in believing that you mean this, Don Carlos."

"Young man," Don Carlos said, "I am too old to start making enemies now. The bad blood between me and your friend is gone—mind you, as long as he stays away from my daughter. You have my word."

"Don Carlos," Clint said, "I will make sure he does just that. On that, you have *my* word."

THIRTY-NINE

Clint rode back into San Sebastian, very satisfied with his meeting with Don Carlos. As it turned out, Witmer had been right not to take the whispers of threats seriously. Clint believed Don Carlos when he said he harbored no ill feelings toward Witmer—at least, none bad enough to wish him dead. Clint was sure that both Witmer and Doc Kennedy would be happy with what he had to report.

He rode Duke to the livery stable and handed him over to the liveryman—who was also new in town since the last time he'd been there.

"You're Mr. Adams, ain't ya?" the man asked.

"That's right."

"I think you better get on over to the Palace right quick."

"Why? What's wrong?"

"Seems your partner got hisself into a high-stakes poker game . . . with a woman!"

"Why is that a problem?" Clint asked. "My partner has been in a lot of high-stakes poker games."

"Seems to me I heard this woman beat him pretty bad a couple of years ago."

Oh, God, Clint thought. It couldn't be, could it?

Lindsey Green was in town?

When Clint walked into the saloon, he knew that what the liveryman had said had to be true. There was a crowd around one table and he could hear poker chips.

"Clint!"

He turned and saw Culley waving to him frantically from behind the bar.

"What's going on?" he asked the bartender.

"You got to stop him, Clint," Culley said. "He's gonna do it again."

"Do what again?"

"He's gonna lose this place to that woman."

"Then it's true? He's playing poker with—"

"Lindsey Green!"

"How did she get here?"

"I think he sent her a telegram," Culley said. "Or maybe she's been reading the papers and she wants to do it to him again. All I know is he wasn't surprised when she showed up."

"Could this have all been to lure her here for a rematch?" Clint asked.

"I wouldn't be surprised if it was. He's never been able to get over the way she beat him last time."

Clint remembered the night before, at dinner, when Witmer said there was still something he had to do before his confidence would be all the way back.

"Is there anyone else in the game?"

"No," Culley said, "they're playing head-to-head. You

gotta stop him. I won't work for that woman!'' The bartender was frantic.

''I'll do what I can, Culley.''

Clint made his way toward the table, having to push through a crowd to get there. When he reached it the first thing he noticed was Lindsey Green's cleavage. It was impressive, and was very much on display. That alone gave him some idea of how she played her game.

''Ken . . .''

''Wait,'' Witmer said, without looking up. They were in the midst of a hand of five-card stud.

''Kenny . . .''

''In a minute, Clint.''

Well, at least Witmer knew he was there.

Clint was surprised to see that the dealer was Holly, the blond girl who had offered to wash his back yesterday. She had some pretty impressive cleavage on display herself. When she looked at Clint, her eyes were pleading.

There were three cards on the table. Witmer had a pair of tens showing, and Lindsey Green was showing an ace and king of spades.

''Your bet, Mr. Witmer,'' Holly said.

''Five hundred.''

''Call,'' the woman said.

Clint examined her face. Her complexion was clear and creamy, her eyes violet. Her hair was black, her full lips were painted red. She appeared to be in her early thirties, and he wondered how they had never managed to meet if she played this kind of poker.

Abruptly, he had to push carnal thoughts from his mind. The woman was trying to take his partner's half of the business away from him and here he was trying to imagine her naked on a bed.

''Fourth card,'' Holly said, and dealt it.

Witmer received a jack of diamonds, and Lindsey Green also got a jack—of spades. She now had three cards to a straight flush.

Witmer took a look at his hole card, which Clint didn't see. All he knew was that his partner was sitting straight up. Was he trying to use the false tell on her, too?

"Mr. Witmer?"

"I know it's my bet, Holly!" he snapped.

"Don't snap at the girl, Kenny," Lindsey Green said.

Witmer gave her a long look and then said, "Five hundred," and pushed the chips into the pot.

"Call," she said with a smile. The woman looked calm and completely unflappable.

"Last card," Holly said, and dealt it.

Witmer got a six of diamonds. If he had no help underneath, all he had was a pair of tens.

Lindsey Green caught the queen of spades. She needed the ten of spades for a straight flush, any spade for a flush, and any ten for a straight. Witmer had two tens, maybe three, so the chance of her catching either straight was slim, but she still had an excellent chance of catching the flush.

Which didn't seem to bother Witmer.

"A thousand."

Clint thought he was crazy to bet a thousand dollars into a four flush.

"Raise a thousand," the woman said with no hesitation.

That's when Clint knew that Witmer had her.

"Reraise," Witmer said.

"You're extraordinarily proud of those tens, Mr. Witmer."

"They're high on the table, Miss Green," Witmer said. "That means I've got to bet them, doesn't it?"

"Well," she said, "I've already waited too long to go with you. The pot is yours."

She folded her four flush without showing her hole card.

Witmer folded his hand over without showing his, as well.

"Take a break," Clint said to Witmer.

"Clint—"

"Take a goddamned break, Kenny!"

"Is this your partner?" Lindsey asked. "The famous Gunsmith?"

"Clint," Witmer said, "this is Miss Lindsey Green. I'm sure you remember me telling you about her."

"I remember," Clint said. "It's a pleasure, Miss Green. Would you mind if I talked to my partner for a moment?"

"Of course not," she said. "I need to recover from that remarkably well played hand anyway."

"Thank you," Clint said, and grabbed Witmer by the elbow. He steered him over to the bar.

"What are you doing?" Clint demanded.

"Just what I was planning on doing all along, Clint."

"So this was all just to get her here?"

"Exactly," Witmer said. "I made sure she knew I had won the poker game, and I also made sure she knew I had a new place. I *knew* she wouldn't be able to resist. I've waited two years to get her at a poker table again, and this time I'm going to take her."

"Or she'll take this place from you."

Witmer patted Clint's arm and said, "If she does that, you'll have a much more beautiful partner."

"And you'll dive back into a bottle."

"No," Witmer said, "I won't. Do you want to know why?"

"Why?"

"Because I'm going to win, Clint," Witmer said, then lowered his voice and said again with conviction, "I'm going to win."

"And why did you need me then, huh?" Clint asked. "If this was what you wanted to do. Why did you need me as a partner?"

"I told you the truth about that, Clint," Witmer said. "I respect you, and I'm afraid of you. I needed you as my partner to make sure I didn't blow this place *before* I got her here."

"So what are you going to do if you win?"

"Oh, I think I'll stay around here for a while," he said, "or I'll go and take a look at my old place."

"What old place?"

"The one she took from me," he said. "I'm gonna take it back."

"You think you're going to get her into a position to put that place on the table?"

"I do," he said. "Her place—my *old* place—against this one."

"How are you going to work that?"

"It'll happen, Clint," Witmer said. "It'll happen all by itself."

"How do you know?"

Witmer touched his nose and said, "Remember this? It smells money. Did you see that last hand?"

"I saw."

"I've got her just where I want her. I only had a pair of tens."

"And she had a four flush. Big deal. Nobody bets a four flush to beat tens."

"I guarantee you she had a higher pair than I did," Witmer said confidently, "but she was convinced I had three tens and that I had her beat."

"The false tell."

"Right."

"Well," Clint said, "it worked on Bat and me. Why wouldn't it work on her?"

"Exactly," Witmer said. "Don't you see, Clint? This is fate. This is what goes around coming around again. Can't you feel it? Even just a little? A little ripple in the air?"

They paused a moment and damned if Clint didn't think he could feel it.

"You do feel it."

Clint nodded.

"Yeah, I guess I do."

"Then shall I go ahead, partner?"

"Sure," Clint said, "do what you've got to do, but get yourself a new dealer."

Witmer frowned.

"Why? Holly's doing well."

"If your luck's going to hold, it'll hold no matter who's dealing, don't you think?"

"I don't think, I know."

"I need Holly."

"What for?"

Clint smiled and said, "I'm going to take a bath."

EPILOGUE

Later Holly was in his lap in the bathtub, his penis buried to the hilt inside of her. They were rocking the tub so much that water was splashing on the floor. He sucked at her slippery breasts while he screwed her, biting the nipples while she raked his back, and then suddenly her eyes went wide and she spasmed and he exploded inside of her. . . .

"Don't you want to be downstairs to see who wins?" she asked later when they had retired to his room to make proper use of the bed.

"No."

"Why not?"

He slid down between her legs and spread her thighs so he could see her blond muff. He blew on it and she wriggled her butt.

"Because Kenny already told me he was going to win," Clint said.

"And you believe him?"

He bent his head and touched her with the tip of his nose. She jerked, as if shocked by lightning.

"He hasn't been wrong yet," Clint said, "not since he came to San Sebastian."

"But . . . ooh, do that again . . . b-but he could be wrong now, couldn't . . . um . . . he?"

"No," Clint said, inhaling the scent of her as she got wet, "he can't."

"Why not?"

"Because," he said, running his tongue up and down her, tasting her, "he's on a winning streak, and it's not over yet."

"Why—oh, screw it—God, don't tease me!" She grabbed his head by the ears and pulled his face against her crotch, and he didn't tease her anymore.

Clint came down hours later, feeling pleasantly fatigued. Holly was asleep in his bed, and he had told her to stay there and wait for him.

The crowd had gone. It was after midnight, and the game was obviously over. Witmer was nowhere to be seen, and neither was the beautiful Lindsey Green.

Clint walked to the bar and told Culley to give him a beer.

"Where's your boss?" Clint asked. "I mean, your other boss?"

"He's in his room."

"Alone?"

"No."

"Celebrating?"

"Oh yeah."

"With who?"

Culley started to laugh.

"Oh, Clint, it was a thing of beauty," Culley said. "The old place isn't all he took from her. He made her bet something else."

"Something else? Like what?"

Culley simply looked upstairs toward Witmer's room.

"You mean . . . she's up there with him?" he asked.

Culley nodded with great satisfaction.

Clint shook his head, raised his mug, and said, "Here's to one *hell* of a winning streak."